"Who the devil are you?"

Diana smothered her scream even as the sound first escaped.

"Well?"

"I am sorry to disturb you, my lord. I only wanted—"

"Who are you?"

"I am your wife, Lord Rossley."

Her blunt response silenced him. With a groan he collapsed back on the mattress.

"May I help you in any way?" she said gently.

"You may leave," came the disagreeable answer.

Diana nodded and slipped from the room. But she couldn't resist one last look at her long-lost husband; it might help her to recognize him when he emerged from the sickroom.

Books by Judith Stafford

HARLEQUIN REGENCY ROMANCE
32—THE LEMON CAKE

A HERO'S WELCOME

JUDITH STAFFORD

Harlequin Books

TORONTO • NEW YORK • LONDON
AMSTERDAM • PARIS • SYDNEY • HAMBURG
STOCKHOLM • ATHENS • TOKYO • MILAN

Published June 1991

ISBN 0-373-31151-6

A HERO'S WELCOME

CHAPTER ONE

BOSWELL WAS GLAD that the Aubusson carpet was thick enough to cushion the teacup's fall. Otherwise, the master's heirloom china service would now be incomplete.

"What did you say?" his mistress asked faintly, her pale cheeks attesting to her shock.

The butler eyed the young woman warily from his hands and knees as he mopped up the remains of the spilt tea. "The master has returned, my lady." His earlier enthusiasm was tempered by her response.

"The war has ended?" Her incredulity was justified, for Napoleon's recent escapades had the British leaders preparing for a long war.

"No, my lady. The master received a wound, requiring him to return home."

The young lady's even white teeth sank into her bottom lip, but she exhibited neither wifely concern nor appreciation for her butler's words.

"Thank you, Boswell. That will be all."

The butler withdrew in his normal stately fashion, closing the double doors of the blue salon behind him.

Diana, Lady Rossley, mistress of Rossley House, sat frozen on the blue silk Egyptian sofa, her mind in turmoil. Lord Rossley had returned? The vague memories she had of the stranger she had married almost a year ago would not permit her to identify him without assistance.

A knock sounded at the parlour door. With swiftly concealed fear, Lady Rossley called, "Enter."

"Mama!"

Holding out her arms in welcome, Lady Rossley hugged the tiny blond whirlwind to her breast, unmindful of her elegant toilette. "Melly, have you come to take tea with me?"

As the four-year-old girl slipped from Lady Rossley's arms to sit beside her with adult decorum, Lady Melanie Rossley nodded with a beaming smile, her curls bouncing. "You promised," she reminded her stepmother.

"Yes, and Cook has sent up a gingerbread man as a special treat, my pet." Before serving the child, she smiled up at the elderly woman who had accompanied the child and was now watching them indulgently. "You may return for her after your tea, Nanny." As the motherly figure turned to leave, Lady Rossley said, "Nanny...Nanny, Lord Rossley has returned."

The incredulous joy which lit up the old woman's face filled Lady Rossley with remorse. *She* should have felt such happiness. But how could she?

"Oh, my lady! How wonderful!"

"Yes, of course." She bent her head to prepare Lady Melanie's tea, ashamed that she did not share the old woman's enthusiasm.

When Nanny returned to collect her charge, Lady Rossley hugged the child to her again, welcoming the warmth. "Go with Nanny, Melly. I will come and sit with you during your supper."

"All right, Mama." The child presented her stepmother with a dignified curtsy before dashing to the door. Diana watched the child's departure with a smile on her lips. For a half hour, she had kept thoughts of her husband's return at bay.

With a sigh, she crossed the room to the bell-pull to summon the butler. She could no longer ignore her husband's return.

"Boswell, has a doctor been called to examine Lord Rossley?" she asked when he appeared.

"Yes, my lady. The Prince Regent's doctor was sent by the Prince himself. He's attending the master now."

"Oh. Would you please ask the doctor to wait upon me when he is finished?"

"Of course, my lady." The butler withdrew and Lady Rossley was alone once more.

She was not prepared for this turn of events. But then, she had not been prepared for the disaster Fate had visited upon her a year ago, either. It was her own inadequacy that had placed her in her present predicament.

A year ago, she had conceded defeat and given up on life. Her father had lost their impoverished estate in a card game and she found herself destitute.

The shock of discovering her father's bloody body sprawled across the desk in the study, pistol in hand, that spring evening had been the culmination of her despair. She had abandoned her hopes and dreams and offered herself up to the soothing depths of the Thames.

"Lady Rossley, Doctor Brownell is here," Boswell announced.

Diana spun round, her hand at her throat. She had been a year and a world away from the elegant sitting-room in Rossley House. Swallowing, she murmured, "Show him in, please, Boswell."

The dapper little man who bowed before her was as elegantly clad as the loftiest nobleman in the land. But his understanding blue eyes twinkled at her, giving Diana confidence in him.

"How is my...Lord Rossley?" she asked, after inviting the man to join her as she returned to the sofa.

"He is a strong man, my lady. They wanted to amputate his arm on the Continent, but he would not let them."

Diana gasped, her hand returning to her throat. "They did not—"

"No, my lady. Lord Rossley and his man prevented their attempts. It is my understanding his man held the surgeons at bay with his lordship's own pistols."

"But his arm—"

"I believe there will be at least partial recovery, my lady. He needs building up, of course, but good English food will make him robust once more."

Diana mumbled a thanks of sorts and the doctor rose, adding, "I'll return tomorrow to guide his recovery."

"That is most kind of you, sir."

"The Prince has a special interest in Lord Rossley. He is a hero, you know. The Duke of Wellington has mentioned him several times in the dispatches." Doctor Brownell beamed down at the lady, sure she joined him in pride of her husband's accomplishments.

"Yes, of course," Diana said faintly.

It appeared word of Lord Rossley's return spread rapidly through the ranks of London Society, for the knocker sounded all afternoon. Though Boswell denied Lady Rossley to acquaintances, he knew better than to do so to Lady Hanson. The elderly woman, her back ramrod straight, demanded sharply as she entered the room, "He's returned?" The trembling of her voice belied her reputed coldness.

Diana rose at once and met her husband's only relative halfway across the room, clasping her hands. "Yes, Aunt Margaret. He's abovestairs. The doctor just left."

"The boy's all right?"

"The doctor said he's very strong."

"Of course he is! He's a Rossley!" The lady sank onto the nearest sofa, the stiff purple taffeta of her dress crackling as she sat. She withdrew a fine lawn handkerchief from her reticule and patted her watery eyes.

Diana sat beside her, offering what comfort she could. She owed much to this warm-hearted woman whom Society considered unfeeling.

"I was so afraid—"

"Mrs. Chadwell, my lady."

Diana had no opportunity to deny herself, even had she wished to, because the diminutive blond lady dressed in the height of fashion appeared before Boswell had finished speaking.

"Oh, Diana, my darling girl! Can it be true? Has our beloved Richard been snatched from the jaws of death and returned to our loving bosoms?"

"Yes..."

"Sit down, Hetta, and stop fluttering," Lady Hanson snapped.

Mrs. Chadwell glared, but sat down, a pout on her lips, and declared, "I do not know how you can be so unfeeling when our dear boy has been returned to us. How is he, Diana? Have you spoken with him? I do so hope he will suffer no ill consequences. I heard that he has sustained a wound and sometimes—"

"Enough!" Lady Hanson pressed her lips tightly together and Diana sighed. Both ladies were important to her and Melanie and she had come to love them. But they were so different in their temperaments.

"Please," she said softly. "The doctor said Lord Rossley will recover, and no, I have not visited him. He is weary from his journey and the...the doctor said it would be best if he were allowed complete rest today." She hoped God would forgive her for that lie. Lady Hanson was the only one who knew the truth behind her marriage. As much as she loved Hetta Chadwell, she knew the woman could no more keep a secret than she could stop breathing.

Lady Hanson nodded and stared reprovingly at Mrs. Chadwell when she would have protested. "Very proper, my dear, putting your husband's needs before your own, and so I shall tell everyone."

"Thank you, Aunt Margaret. I shall, of course, inform him of your concern for his welfare, and I'm sure he will be grateful."

"He won't be grateful for mine," Mrs. Chadwell said as she sniffed.

There was no need for explanation to the other two ladies, for they were well aware of Lord Rossley's feelings towards Mrs. Chadwell. As the mother of his first wife, Mrs. Chadwell had received much of the blame when his adored Alicia had shown herself to be unworthy of his youthful idealism.

"In fact, if he were not abed, I'm sure he would show me the door at once." The tears flowed copiously from her pale blue eyes.

Diana exchanged a wry look with Lady Hanson. This conversation had taken place several times in the past year. "Now, Hetta," Diana pleaded, "don't cry. You know Melly could not bear it if her Grandma Hetta were not allowed to take her on outings."

"I must say," Lady Hanson added in her brisk fashion, "much to my surprise, you make an admirable grandmother. Richard would be a fool to deny you. It just may...may take a little longer to make him realize it. But neither Diana nor I will abandon your cause."

"Oh, Margaret, thank you," Mrs. Chadwell cried. "With you on my side, I know Richard will forgive me."

Diana smiled ruefully. Even though Mrs. Chadwell did not know the true story behind their marriage, it was clear she gave little credence to Diana's powers over her husband.

"Come," Lady Hanson said, rising. "It is time we left this poor child alone. She has much to deal with." Her firm stare brought Hetta Chadwell gracefully to her feet. Once she was assured of Hetta's compliance, she turned back to Diana, who had also risen. "We shall return tomorrow to discover how my great-nephew is faring. Send word if you have need of me before then."

Diana bestowed a kiss on that forbidding brow, bringing a rare smile to Lady Hanson's face. "Thank you, Aunt Margaret. As always, I do not know what I would do without you."

"You would manage, child. You are almost as strong as the Rossleys. A perfect mate for Richard." Her statement left no room for argument and Diana said nothing, only bidding Hetta goodbye as well.

A perfect mate for Richard. *Richard?* She had called the man nothing but Lord Rossley the two times she had seen him. The night he rescued her was a blur, but she believed he had introduced himself to her before sending her to bed in Mrs. Boswell's care.

The next day, he had convinced her to marry him. In truth, it did not take much persuasion. She had not recovered from the previous day's devastation and would have agreed to almost any way out of her predicament.

The words were scarcely out of her mouth when he had produced a special licence, a clergyman and his man of business. The marriage was over in a matter of seconds, or so it seemed to Diana, and she was turned over to the care of the Boswells and Mr. Wilson, Lord Rossley's man of business. It was only later that she discovered her husband had signed a power of attorney, giving her full charge of his three-year-old daughter.

"My lady, Mr. Edward White and Sir Robert Bruce are below. They want information about the master."

Diana read the concern in the servant's face and smiled in gratitude. Boswell and his wife had helped her through those first dreadful days, earning her undying gratitude. "Please show them up, Boswell."

The two gentlemen were old friends of her husband's and had made her transition into Society easier by the friendship they extended to her. Edward's wife, Sara, had become her best friend.

Edward White was of medium height, his sandy hair and smiling face a trademark of his easygoing nature. He and Sara were favourites among the ton. Sir Robert Bruce had a dark, brooding look and, since his return from the war, had been much compared to Byron, despite his protests. Diana knew it was his limp that made him hate such a comparison. He considered himself less than a man because he could not walk like others.

In truth, the limp was only slight, limiting his dancing but little else. Diana and Sara and Edward had done their best to reassure him, but he continued to avoid social events. Now, he strode into the room ahead of Edward, impatient for news.

"Is it true?" he asked, coming over to the sofa where Diana sat.

"Yes, Robert, it is true." She looked beyond the tall man to greet Edward. "Please, sit down. Boswell, would you bring us a tea tray?"

"How is he?" Edward asked, his warm smile a support to Diana's shaky nerves.

"The doctor said he is very strong. They...they wanted to amputate his arm, but he would not let them."

"God, no!"

"We would have welcomed him back, arm or no arm, Robert," Edward admonished his friend. "But I'm glad he did not suffer that."

"Yes," Diana agreed fervently. "The Prince's own doctor came and said he will recover, though he is not sure his arm will...will be as before."

"Another debt Boney owes us," Robert said bitterly.

Diana said nothing, only covering Robert's clenched fist with her soft hand.

"That is wonderful, Diana," Edward declared, but his eyes focussed on their clasped hands. "By the way, Sara and Clare send their love."

Diana flashed a look at Robert at the mention of Sara's sister, but his face showed nothing.

"Please thank them for me, Edward."

"They wanted to accompany us, of course, but I thought you might not be prepared to entertain."

With a rueful smile, Diana said, "I am not, but I do not consider visits from friends in that light. I am sure R-Richard will be warmed to know of your love and concern."

"When may we see him?" Robert demanded.

Diana withdrew her hand to rearrange the folds of her peach muslin gown. "The doctor said he should have no visitors today. I will ask him how soon you may see Richard when he comes back tomorrow." It was dismaying how much more easily the lies came when they were told a second time.

"Of course," Edward said. "We did not expect to visit with Richard today. But you will tell him we were anxious to see him?"

"Of course I will, Edward. I'm sure it will cheer him immensely to know of such loyal friends."

Both men smiled. Edward added, "We are loyal, but none of us are much good at writing letters. We have had only three letters between us since he left a little over a year ago, and they told us of nothing but soldiering. I hope you have fared better."

Though she knew Edward was not attempting to pry, Diana's cheeks flooded in embarrassment. There had been no communication between her husband and herself since their wedding day.

Edward, misinterpreting her blush, exclaimed, "Ah! Obviously your letters dealt with more personal matters than troop movements."

Diana only smiled and was grateful that Boswell returned with the tea tray at that moment. She busied herself dispensing the tea. Once all three of them had been served, she desperately sought a safe topic.

Robert, however, wanted to discuss the man above-stairs. "I wonder how much the war has changed him?" His audience didn't appear disposed to answer. "You do understand, don't you, Diana, that Richard may not be quite himself for a while?"

Hysterical laughter bubbled up in Diana and she took a sip of tea to quell it. How would *she* know whether the man was himself or not? She nodded, hoping a silent answer would satisfy Robert.

"I know you were not married long before his departure, and it is not fair that your reunion should be under such circumstances, but... but it is difficult to adjust to civilian life after..." He trailed off, his eyes staring into space at a world Diana could never hope to understand.

Reaching over to pat his hand again, she said softly, "It is all right, Robert. I shall be patient."

"Of course you shall, Diana. Look at how you won Melanie's heart," Edward said in encouraging tones.

Smiling her thanks, Diana offered her guests more tea, but both gentlemen refused and stood to leave. Hoping she hid her gratitude for the brevity of their stay, Diana rose also.

"You will let us know if there is anything we may do to assist you?" Edward asked.

"Yes, of course, and tell Sara and Clare I am grateful for their good wishes."

"May they call on you tomorrow?"

"I would be delighted to see them, and both of you also, if you would care to escort them. The doctor is to return in the morning, and I will ask him about your visiting Richard. I am sure your concern will be good medicine for him."

"Then we shall come, also," Edward assured her after a quick look at his companion.

Robert took her hand and drew it to his lips. "Until tomorrow, Diana."

"Yes," Diana replied simply, and remained standing until the two gentlemen had departed. Then she collapsed onto the sofa. The events of the day had drained her of all her normal vivacity and energy.

"My lady," Nanny said as she opened the door, "Lady Melanie is waiting for you." She paused, viewing the young woman, and hurried forward. "Are you quite well, my lady?"

Diana struggled to her feet, meeting the elderly woman's outstretched hands with her own. "Yes, of course, Nanny. Lord Rossley's return has... has been a surprise, that's all. I'll come at once."

DIANA SLIPPED from the nursery after an enthusiastic good-night kiss from her stepdaughter. With a sigh, she wandered down the stairs, feeling but little interest in the evening before her. She had already decided that to appear at Mrs. Hazelwood's musicale would give rise to the wrong kind of speculation about her husband's return. She would write a brief note excusing herself.

As she entered her rooms, her eyes were drawn immediately to the connecting door to the master suite. She had gone into Lord Rossley's bedchamber several times in the past year. Once, out of curiosity, she had slipped in, hoping to find something that would tell her about the man whose name she bore. Then, about three months ago, Mrs. Boswell had asked about including his rooms in the annual cleaning she gave the house before the Season started. Diana had concurred and had supervised the maids.

But it was not cleanliness that drew Diana now. She was intensely curious about the man who occupied those rooms.

Without further thought, Diana walked over and cautiously opened the door. The dressing-room showed signs of new occupation. The dust covers had been removed from what little furniture was there, and there were several travelling bags sitting open in one corner.

Since the valet was not present, Diana drew a deep breath and inched her way across the room to an identical door on the other side. Very slowly she pushed it open.

There was only one candle lit in the dim room. The curtains were drawn and there was a fire burning in the grate. Diana could discern no movement. Unable to resist, she tiptoed forward towards the huge bed that dominated the room.

Its draperies were tied back for easy access to the feather bed covered with the finest linens. There was a form in the centre of the bed that must have been Lord Rossley. Diana stood-stock still, her breathing shallow and rapid. After a moment, when there was still no movement, Diana moved stealthily forward and leaned over the bed to peer down at this stranger who was her husband.

"Who the devil are you?"

CHAPTER TWO

DIANA SMOTHERED her scream even as the sound first escaped. With trembling legs she backed away from the figure that had suddenly risen up to accost her.

"Well?"

Diana noticed several things at once. She had thought she could not remember anything about her husband, but his voice awoke memories in her—and it also told her he was exhausted and as fretful as Melly when she had a cold.

That realization gave her courage and she said softly, "I am sorry to disturb you, my lord. I only wanted—"

"Who *are* you?"

"I am your wife, Lord Rossley."

Her blunt response silenced him. With a groan he collapsed back onto the mattress.

"May I help you in any way?"

There was silence. Diana leaned forward again and could see that his eyes were closed. She jumped when they opened and he stared at her. "Where is Dawson?"

She knew from Boswell that Dawson was her husband's valet, but she had never met him. "I—I do not know. Shall I find him?"

"Yes."

She backed away, unable to take her eyes from the man who had saved her life and given it new meaning, even though he was a stranger. Unaware of the door opening behind her, she squealed in fright as she bumped into another person.

"I'm sorry, miss," the man muttered, an underlying question in his apology.

"You must be Dawson," she whispered. "I am Lady Rossley. Your master needs you."

With punctilious politeness, the servant bowed. "Yes, Lady Rossley. I shall attend to him at once."

"Is there—is there anything I can do to assist you?"

The man looked over her shoulder and then shook his head. "Thank you, my lady, but the master just needs to rest."

Diana nodded and slipped from the room. But she couldn't resist one last look at her long-lost husband; it might help her to recognize him when he emerged from the sickroom.

THE NEXT MORNING, Diana reached the breakfast table early. As Boswell served her, she said, "Please let me know when Doctor Brownell arrives, Boswell, and ask him to wait upon me when he has seen Lord Rossley."

"Yes, my lady."

She wanted to ask the man if he had been to see his master, but she refrained. Boswell was a long-time

family retainer, a footman in Lord Rossley's youth.
One thing she had discovered about the absent Lord
Rossley's household: in spite of his strange behaviour, he was greatly loved and respected among his
servants.

She munched on a piece of toast, her thoughts occupied with her husband's arrival. Would her life
change again? In only a year, she had travelled from
abject despair to happiness. She owed it all to Lord
Rossley: not only had he provided her with all the finery her heart desired, but he had also given her a child
to love. With Lady Hanson, Mrs. Chadwell, Melanie
and her friends, she was surrounded by love and
comfort. She had much for which to be grateful.

Boswell re-entered the breakfast parlour. "My lady,
Lord Rossley requests that you wait upon him at your
earliest convenience."

Diana's eyes widened in surprise. Her first thought
was of her appearance, though she was not a vain
woman. Her pale blue sprigged muslin was the ulti-
mate in fashion. Her hair, dressed in curls and pulled
back from her oval face, was a plain brown, a fact
much lamented by Diana. Though she had dressed it
this morning in a matching blue ribbon, she thought
it uninteresting when compared to Melly's golden
locks.

She wiped the crumbs of the toast from her gown
and stood up. "Do—do I appear to advantage, Boswell?"

"In every way, my lady," the elderly man assured
her, a warm smile on his face.

"You always say that, Boswell," Diana said with a smile, her nervousness dissipating somewhat with his kindness.

"Because it is always true. His lordship is a fortunate man."

Diana only smiled in return. It would be senseless to argue, but she doubted that Lord Rossley would feel the same way. Drawing a deep breath, she marched up the stairs to her interview with her husband.

The bedchamber was well lit this morning by the large window on the front of the house, facing east. The draperies were pulled back to allow the light to seek out even the remote corners. Diana didn't stop to admire the view, however. Her interest was centred in the large bed.

Bright blue eyes stared at her, and she swept a deep curtsy before sinking into the chair placed beside the bed. Dawson excused himself, pulling the door of the dressing-room to behind him, and Diana was alone with her husband.

Lord Rossley was propped up on numerous pillows and the light revealed his thin and haggard face. Even with the ravages of war on his brow, Diana thought him a handsome man, his blond hair much like Melly's. His eyes, however, were much sharper than his daughter's. Melanie had china-blue eyes that gave her an innocent appeal even when she was at her naughtiest, while Lord Rossley's eyes were a piercing blue. Diana would not want to face them with a guilty conscience.

"Madam, I apologize for my harsh words of last evening."

Snapped from her thoughts, Diana felt her cheeks flush. "It is of no moment, my lord. I should not have entered your chamber without your leave."

Silence fell as his eyes left her to stare into space. Diana did not know whether to offer social chatter or remain silent. Her husband took that choice from her. With bitter irony in his voice, he said, "I also apologize for my unexpected return."

Diana stared at him, recalling their wedding day. *"Do not concern yourself with our marriage, my dear. You will be fitted for widow's weeds before long."* Those had been his last words to her before she was dismissed to her room. He had left the house within the hour and she had not seen him again until the previous night, more than a year later.

"The entire household is celebrating your safe return, my lord, as well as your many friends. No apology is necessary." His response to her words was a scowl so like Melly's that Diana had to hide her smile.

"Do not try to convince me you are pleased by my return," he growled.

"You must think me a monster, my lord. You saved my life and have provided for me most generously. I am delighted that you have returned home."

"God's blood, woman! Must you sound so saintly?"

A chuckle rose from deep within her. "I will do my best to appear more villainous."

He eyed her sharply. "I do not see the comedy in our situation."

"And I do not see the tragedy, my lord," she returned simply. "We are both intelligent beings, with many of the world's luxuries at our command. If we cannot make the best of it, then the fault is in ourselves.''

He turned away from her and for the first time, Diana noticed a look of distress on his face. ''Your arm pains you?''

''Every damn moment!''

When she remained silent, he added roughly, ''I apologize for my language.''

''I have heard worse, my lord. The doctor intended to return this morning, but I shall have Boswell send for him at once.''

''No! There is little he can do.'' He closed his eyes, and Diana sat quietly, wondering if he would fall asleep. ''How old are you?'' he asked, his eyes still closed.

''I just turned twenty, my lord, this week past.''

He opened his eyes and stared at her. ''You have a great deal of composure for one so young.''

''Lady Hanson is an excellent teacher,'' she said, her eyes lowered demurely.

''Aunt Margaret?'' When she only nodded, he asked, ''What has Aunt Margaret to do with you?''

''When she discovered me in residence, she was kind enough to sponsor me in Society.''

''I find that difficult to believe, unless you hoodwinked my aunt.'' His hard tones were reflected in his eyes.

''No, my lord, I told Aunt Margaret the truth.''

''What? How dare you! I did not intend...'' His voice trailed off and he avoided her eye.

"I am sorry if I did not behave as you wished, but you left me with no instructions."

"So, you have been draining the estates to pay for your finery and parading around at all the parties. And have you taken many lovers since my departure?"

Diana had heard the rumours about Alicia, the former Lady Rossley. Finally, she had asked Sara to tell her the truth about the woman who had given birth to her beloved Melly. Shortly before Lord Rossley discovered Diana in the Thames, Alicia had died in a carriage accident with her lover as they made for the Continent. She didn't need the pain in Lord Rossley's voice to tell her his first wife had hurt him deeply. With a gentle smile, she said, "No, my lord. Your good name has been safe with me."

His cheeks flushed and he turned away. "I do not care. Do what you will!"

Diana's smile widened. Before she could respond, however, the door opened.

Dawson bowed to her before turning to his master. "Doctor Brownell has arrived, my lord."

Diana rose. "I shall await the doctor's report downstairs. Please inform me if I can assist your recovery in any way." With a slight curtsy, she left the room.

THE DOCTOR'S REPORT was much more favourable than that of the previous afternoon. Even one day's rest from the torturous trip from the Continent had done much to restore Lord Rossley. Knowing Lady Hanson would be anxious to see her beloved nephew,

Diana had gained permission for her to visit the sick-room. All others were to be turned away for now, however. The doctor did not want Lord Rossley to tire himself.

When Lady Hanson arrived, she was beside herself with excitement; her features were unusually ani-mated and she climbed the stairs with the vigour of youth. Diana escorted her to her husband's chamber herself, but she had no intention of remaining with them.

"Where are you going?" Lord Rossley demanded as she walked towards the door. His aunt had enthu-siastically greeted him and taken possession of one of the chairs pulled up to the bed.

Diana turned in surprise. "I was returning to the parlour, my lord."

"No. You'll stay," he ordered peremptorily. "I must hear what you told my aunt."

A whimsical smile touched Diana's shapely lips. "You do not trust Aunt Margaret to tell you?"

His eyes hardened in a look Diana was coming to know quite well. "I believe my aunt will tell the truth. But I want you present."

"Very well, my lord," Diana replied, and returned to take the chair beside Lady Hanson.

"You shouldn't address him by his title among family, my dear," Lady Hanson said in an instructive fashion, ignoring the fuming man.

"Yes, Aunt Margaret. The difficulty is that he has not given me permission to use his first name and I am reluctant to do so until he does."

"Nonsense, child. That permission comes with the marriage licence. It is your right."

"If you intend to ignore my presence, you might as well both descend to the parlour," Lord Rossley said stiffly, staring straight ahead.

"Here now, boy, there's no need to get on your high horse. I am merely preparing Diana for the time you are in company." His aunt's calm response only exacerbated Lord Rossley's temper.

"If we are in company, we shall not be among family." Lord Rossley's eyes swung towards his wife, distracted by her laughter. "What do you find so amusing, madam?"

"I am sorry, my—Richard. I did not mean to offend."

"Of course not," Lady Hanson interrupted. "The child has a delightful sense of humour. Have you noticed the change in Melly? She laughs just like her stepmama." The pride in Lady Hanson's voice seemed to indicate that she was responsible for such a change.

"Melly? I had not thought—" Lord Rossley broke off, his teeth sinking into his firm bottom lip. "Have you told her I have returned?"

"No, Richard. I thought it best to wait until you are more fully recovered. She will be anxious to see you and will not understand the delay." Diana smiled, pleased with his interest in his child. "She is a delightful little girl. I am so grateful you trusted her to me."

"Abandoned her, more like!" Lady Hanson snorted. "I've a bone to pick with you, nephew, about your departure last year. It turned out all right, because Diana's a right 'un, but it might well have been a disaster!''

''I had no choice. *You* refused to care for her,'' Lord Rossley said accusingly.

''Course I did. Hoped it would bring you to your senses. Instead, the next thing I know, you're gone and your child has been left to a stranger.'' Lady Hanson reached over to pat Diana's hand. ''Fine girl. I've come to love her, but that's not the point.''

Diana read the strain and exhaustion in her husband's face and knew the past had best be left buried until another day. ''Aunt Margaret, I believe Boswell has our tea waiting for us in the parlour.''

''What? But I want—'' The lady broke off as Diana gestured to her husband. ''Eh? Oh, of course, of course.'' She stood and bent over the bed to give the surprised young man a kiss on his forehead. ''You rest now, boy. I'll return tomorrow.''

''There's no need to put yourself out,'' he grumbled, glaring at his wife.

''I'm sure Aunt Margaret will be unable to stay away after that gracious remark,'' Diana teased with a smile that drew no answering response from her husband.

''Send Dawson to me.''

After alerting the valet of their departure, the two ladies descended the stairs in silence. Once they were seated in the parlour, Lady Hanson sipped her tea with a frown.

''Is your tea not to your liking, Aunt Margaret?''

''What? Oh, of course it is, child. Boswell knows exactly how I like my tea.'' She took another sip before returning the cup to the tea table. "It's Richard. He's sadly pulled by this wound. Are you sure the doctor is capable?"

"He is the Prince Regent's own doctor, Aunt Margaret. Besides, I like him."

"Hmm. Very well, child. I trust your judgement. But we must build up his strength. He used to have such a sunny disposition."

Diana hid her smile behind her teacup. After sipping her tea, she said, "He reminds me so much of Melly when she does not feel well."

"There is a lot of her father in that darling child. A good thing, too, or he might not have believed she was his!"

"Aunt Margaret!"

"Don't go playing the schoolroom miss for my benefit, young lady. You know what that woman was like." A ferocious frown marked Lady Hanson's brow. "She almost ruined Richard's life."

Boswell interrupted their tête-à-tête. "Mr. and Mrs. White, Miss Seaton and Sir Robert Bruce have called, my lady."

"Do you mind if we receive them, Aunt Margaret? They are anxious for news of Richard."

"Of course not, child. They have been good allies." When Lady Hanson first launched Diana into Society, she had found her nephew's friends ready to rally round his wife. It had made their campaign so much more successful.

"Please show them up, Boswell."

Sara White and her sister, Clare, were Diana's closest friends. While Diana and Clare were almost of an age, she discovered she had more in common with Sara simply because she was not participating in the marriage mart and because she had the responsibility for Melanie. Sara, the mother of three small children, was able to give Diana much good counsel on the rearing of children.

Diana rose to greet her friends, including the gentlemen with a smile. They each acknowledged Lady Hanson's presence before being seated.

"How is Richard?" Edward asked at once.

"Sadly pulled by his experience, but better after a night's rest in his own bed," Diana said calmly.

"May we see him?" Sir Robert demanded, leaning forward intently.

"Oh, Robert, I am afraid not yet. The doctor says he must rebuild his strength. Aunt Margaret visited for only a few minutes, and already Richard showed signs of exhaustion."

"But his arm?"

Diana knew Robert's concern stemmed from his own disability. Before his injury, Sir Robert Bruce had been known for his prowess in all sports, his lithe grace and manly form much admired among the ladies. She smiled at him. "I do not know, my friend. The doctor is not sure how well he will recover."

"But we are so grateful he is returned to us," Sara said quietly.

"If he were my husband, it would not matter if he were... if he had an injury. He is a hero!" Clare declared passionately, blushing when all eyes save one person's focussed on her.

Sir Robert stared at his boots, saying nothing.

"Of course, girl," Lady Margaret said warmly. "He's a hero. And his wife's delighted he's returned, ain't you, Diana?"

"I am very happy, Aunt Margaret."

"Have you told Lady Melanie?" Sara asked.

"Not yet. I thought I would wait until Richard has more strength. She will not understand the delay in visiting her papa."

"Do you think she will remember him?" Edward asked.

"Oh, yes. Richard spent a great deal of time with her when . . . before he left for the war."

Everyone avoided the subject of Melanie's mother. After an awkward pause, Clare introduced the topic of last night's musicale, telling of Lord Broome who fell asleep during a pianoforte recital and snored loudly. Her sister assisted her in distracting the others with more stories.

When the visitors rose to leave, along with Lady Hanson, Diana was in a cheerful frame of mind. Life was so much more wonderful than it was a year ago, and she was optimistic that all would turn out well.

"Will you come to the Malverns' ball this evening?" Sir Robert asked as they were leaving.

Diana frowned. "I do not know, Robert. There is little I can do for Richard, but I do not want to appear heartless." The spectre of his first wife's reputation rose again. "I believe I shall stay at home for a few days, until Richard is more on the road to recovery."

"We shall call each day to bring you the news so you will not feel too isolated," Clare promised.

"Good. And I feel sure the doctor will permit Richard a few visitors shortly."

"If his mood has not improved, few visitors will be all he will have," Lady Hanson grumbled.

Edward laughed. "Richard was never a good patient, my lady. Do you not remember when he broke his ankle in a hunting accident?"

The elderly lady chuckled. "Lord, yes. He almost drove his mother crazy."

"As soon as he may have visitors, we shall relieve you of the ogre's company as much as possible, Diana, though he probably will not be as difficult with you." Edward slapped his friend on the back. "I have much experience with a difficult invalid. I spent time with Robert after *his* return."

"And I have much experience withstanding Edward's detestable cheerfulness," Robert added, grimacing at his friend. "Richard will need me."

"I'm sure he will depend on the two of you completely," Diana said, "and I am grateful for such good friends."

Boswell appeared to escort the guests to the door. As Diana stood awaiting their departure, he whispered, "The master is asking to see Lady Melanie, my lady."

Diana nodded and turned a serene countenance to speed her guests, but underneath she wondered how to deal with her husband's demand.

CHAPTER THREE

SHE SLIPPED into the chamber quietly, but even so, the man occupying the large bed was aware of her arrival.

"Why are you here?" he demanded.

"Boswell said you were asking to see Melly. I want to ensure that you were not too tired for a child's exertions."

"I suppose I may see my child when I wish," he said belligerently.

"Of course you may, Richard," Diana replied soothingly, as if speaking to a fretful child. "But Melly will be very excited when I tell her her papa has returned. We have spoken of you often while you were gone."

"You have?"

His surprise amused her. "Melly loves you very much."

"But I told you I would not be coming back."

Diana pulled a chair close to the bed and sat down. "When you left, Richard, I was shocked by... by my father's death and worried about my future. I don't think I even understood what you said to me then."

He turned his head away from her. "I did not mean to take advantage of you."

Diana smiled gently and reached out to touch his hand which was lying on the coverlet. He jumped as if she had pinched him. "I do not think either of us were rational, Richard, but I have no regrets. You gave me back my life, and you gave me Melly to love. I received the best part of our bargain."

"You are not angry with me?"

"It would be the height of ingratitude to be angry for such generosity. Now, are you sure you have the strength to take on your daughter today? She is perfectly happy and will be just as pleased to see her papa tomorrow."

He sighed as he fidgeted with the cover. "I do not know. But suddenly I felt so guilty for having abandoned her, as Aunt Margaret said—"

"You must not let her words disturb you. Let's wait until tomorrow before you visit with Melly. I promise to bring her at your earliest request."

"Very well," he agreed with a sigh. As if released from a great worry, he slowly closed his eyes. Diana sat quietly by the bed until his even breathing told her he had slipped into sleep. She rose and tapped lightly on the dressing-room door.

"Dawson?"

"Yes, my lady?" the valet said, appearing at once.

"Your master is asleep. We shall save Lady Melanie's visit for another day."

"But the master will be upset, my lady. He specifically requested her to come to his chamber."

"I know, Dawson, but after talking with me, he agreed to wait until tomorrow. Should he change his mind, you have only to send for me." With a smile, she left the room.

Dawson stared after her in wonder. His master could have commanded his life and received it in a moment's notice, but he didn't mind admitting he preferred not to cross him. It seemed the new mistress had a rare courage, or a rare talent for handling difficult invalids.

"DAMN!" Lord Rossley yanked the stiff white cravat from around his neck and threw it on the floor to join numerous others. He was finding it impossible to turn himself out in the accepted style with only one useful arm.

The door opened and Dawson halted in surprise. "My lord!" He rushed over to his master's side, protest written all over his countenance. "The doctor did not agree to your dressing."

"Damn the doctor! Damn all doctors! I will do what I please, Dawson!" Lord Rossley grabbed the one remaining cravat and slung it round his neck, its snowy whiteness a contrast to his anger-reddened skin.

Dawson set aside the tray he was carrying and approached his master with trepidation. "May I, my lord?"

Though his first response was an emphatic no, Lord Rossley sighed and surrendered the cravat to his valet. Dawson had stayed by his side through many difficulties. He did not deserve his anger. "Sorry, Dawson. But I cannot bear being cooped up in this room any longer."

"I'm sure Lady Rossley would welcome you downstairs in your dressing gown, my lord. A most understanding lady, she is."

Rossley pressed his lips together, staring stonily ahead. He had no complaints about his wife. She had been all that was accommodating since his return. In fact, it was that perfection which was driving him insane. The servants sang her praises; his aunt harped on how well he had chosen his bride; his friends assumed he loved her as much as they.

For three weeks, he had heard nothing but adulation of Lady Rossley. He was congratulated for his wisdom in choosing so wisely. While no one referred directly to his first wife, the implication was clear.

"I have no intention of stopping downstairs. I shall take a turn in the Park." Dawson's eyes widened and he opened his mouth to protest, but Lord Rossley forestalled him. "No, I shall not try to drive. I am not an idiot!"

"No, my lord, of course not." Dawson busied himself with the intricate task of properly tying the cravat. When he had finished and stood back to admire his work, he asked, "Shall I inform Lady Rossley? I'm sure she'll be delighted to accompany you."

Lord Rossley brows snapped together and he stared at his valet. "Why would you suggest such a thing?"

Dawson bent down to pick up the discarded cravats, mumbling, "Her ladyship has stayed at home since your return. No doubt she longs for an outing, too."

Several responses rushed through Lord Rossley's mind, but he was a fair man. His wife had been exemplary in difficult circumstances. "Very well, Dawson. Convey my compliments to my wife and request her company on my drive in the Park. And have the stables send round the brougham with my matched greys."

As soon as Dawson had eased his blue superfine jacket on him, the valet slipped from the room to do his master's bidding. Richard stood staring morosely at himself in the mirror. One couldn't detect his infirmity when he was at rest. But any movement required a monumental effort. Did he have the courage to expose himself to the ton?

He had never avoided facing up to anything, he assured himself stoutly—until he remembered his abrupt departure to war the previous year. He turned away from the mirror. He didn't want to think about that decision or the fruits of it, which haunted him now.

"Lady Rossley is pleased to join you, my lord," Dawson said breathlessly as he entered the room.

"Of course she is," Richard muttered to himself. The woman did whatever she was supposed to do, without any protests. For three weeks, she had met his every need with the greatest of ease and put up with his foul temper in the bargain. Was she inhuman?

"Very well, Dawson. Thank you. I'll await Lady Rossley in the front parlour." Already tired from his efforts to dress, Richard walked gingerly down the stairs and entered the parlour, taking a seat in one of the wing-chairs by the fireplace. With a sigh he leaned his head back. Would he ever regain the strength and energy he had once taken for granted? He had been an active member in the Four-in-Hand Club, ridden to hounds all winter, and danced the spring away with the loveliest of ladies. Now the mere act of dressing and descending to the parlour took his breath away.

DIANA SETTLED HER NEWEST bonnet on her carefully arranged ringlets, tied the ribbon beneath her chin and surveyed her appearance in the mirror. Would Lord Rossley find her acceptable? She could never compare to his first wife's beauty. The portrait of the first Lady Rossley had haunted her since her marriage. And she had Melly's beauty to give it life.

Ah, well. In the past year, she had learned to count her blessings. She only hoped Lord Rossley felt so inclined. It was a sign of progress that he was ready to leave his bedchamber. The doctor was encouraged by his rapid recovery, though his arm was not mending as quickly as the rest of him.

She had attended the sickroom many times in the past three weeks, but she knew little more about her husband now than she had when he first returned home.

"Lord Rossley is awaiting you in the front parlour, my lady," Cassie, her maid, informed her as she slipped into the room.

"Thank you, Cassie. I'll go down at once."

THEIR PROGRESS through the Park was at a snail's pace. Not only was the traffic heavy as always, but also everyone wanted to extend congratulations to the latest returned hero. Lord Rossley was being acclaimed by the Prince Regent himself as a man of rare courage.

Diana watched the handsome man beside her out of the corner of her eye. In his elegant clothes, basking in the sun's brightness, he seemed so much more vital. His vivid blue eyes surveyed the scene before him as if he had never been away.

"Did you...did you miss life in London?" she asked.

Lord Rossley turned to look at his wife. She had been remarkably silent during their ride. It had been his experience that ladies of fashion expected constant flattery and attention, but she had proved him wrong. "No."

When she turned away from his abrupt answer, he added, "I never liked the slow pace of the afternoon parade in Hyde Park. Do you enjoy it?"

"Occasionally," she replied, sending him a grateful smile for his concession. "Sometimes I bring Melly. She loves all the bright colours and the horses. She has been pestering me to learn to ride."

Lord Rossley frowned. "After the Season, we must return to Rossfield, where my head groom will instruct her."

"You should tell her. She will be thrilled," Diana assured him even as she nodded at an acquaintance.

They continued on in silence for a time before Richard said abruptly, "You have taken good care of Melly. I am grateful."

Diana's arched brows rose in surprise. "You have nothing to thank me for, Richard. I love Melly. She is a darling."

"Most young women do not care to be bothered with a child when there are parties to attend."

They both felt the shadow of his first wife, but Diana refused to acknowledge it. "I enjoy my time spent with Melly. I was an only child myself."

He noted the smile on her face. She was no diamond, but her expressive features carried a warmth and intelligence which he found appealing. Then his thoughts were interrupted by another acquaintance.

"Oh, Lord Rossley, how thrilled we are to see you," the woman cooed, leaning forward from her carriage.

"Thank you, Mrs. Atherton," Richard responded coolly. He thought the woman might fall if she leaned any further. When he would have turned back to his wife, the woman called, "You have not met my Melissa. Is she not a beauty?" Reaching out to pull forward the young woman beside her, she waited for the hero's approbation.

"How do you do, Miss Atherton? May I present my wife, Lady Rossley?" The women all exchanged greetings, though Mrs. Atherton's was somewhat cool.

"Miss Atherton is quite beautiful," Diana said calmly as they passed on.

"Yes, and turned out in fine style to catch herself a rich husband." His bored drawl held more than a trace of bitterness.

Diana hesitated, but finally said, "It is not Miss Atherton's fault that she seeks a rich husband. It is the fault of Society, my lord."

"What do you mean?" Lord Rossley asked sharply.

"What choice does a woman have? She has no means to care for herself. Property is entailed to the oldest son. There are few if any occupations open to her, and for hard labour she receives only a pittance. If that were your future, would you not barter your face for a fortune?''

Lord Rossley stared at the female beside him. ''So you approve of the husband-hunting that goes on during the Season?''

Diana wished she had kept her thoughts to herself. But she could not stop now. ''Approval is a strong word, my lord, but I can at least say that I understand the reasons for it.''

''A man would have too much honour.''

''You mean men never marry for a fortune?''

Richard squirmed in his seat. He did not like the direction this conversation was taking. ''*I* would not.''

''Perhaps you have never been faced with poverty,'' Diana murmured quietly.

Much to Richard's relief, they were interrupted once more, this time by Sara and Edward, accompanied by Clare. Both Rossleys greeted their friends eagerly.

''We did not know you were venturing out into Society, Richard,'' Sara said gaily.

''Just a brief foray for fresh air,'' he assured his friend's wife. Sara had long been a favourite of his.

''Rob will be pleased when—'' Edward began.

''Richard! My poor dear Richard! I am so thrilled to see you out of the sickroom. They have prohibited me from visiting you, but of course my heart has been with you! What a relief to know that you have recovered,'' The trilling voice that intruded into their conversation turned Lord Rossley to stone and made his wife wish she had stayed at home.

In spite of the fact that Mrs. Chadwell knew her former son-in-law blamed her for his disaster of a marriage and had forbidden her his house before he left Town, she could not hold back her feelings.

"Good day, Mrs. Chadwell," Richard said coldly before turning back to his friends.

Diana watched as Hetta Chadwell's enthusiasm flew away and her face crumpled in pain. "Oh, Richard! Please do not remain angry with me. Truly—"

Her plea was halted by Lord Rossley's icy words. "I have no desire to converse with you, madam. I believe I made myself clear on that head some months previously."

Diana's eyes held sympathy but she said nothing, bowing her head as Mrs. Chadwell's carriage moved on. After an awkward moment, conversation was resumed among the group, but Diana took no part in it.

As they pulled away from their friends, Diana noted the weariness showing on her husband's face. She quietly leaned forward and directed their coachman to leave by the nearest gate and take them home.

"I'll have you know, madam, I am not a child to be cosseted and coddled, with no say in my life."

Diana looked into the sharp blue eyes in which stubborn pride glowed, and remarked mildly, "I beg your pardon, my lord, but I thought you would not mind cutting short your first outing. While you have fared quite well, I have a blinding headache which makes continuing impossible."

Though he stared at her, she calmly leaned her head back against the comfortable leather seat and closed her eyes, remaining thus until they drew up before their residence.

Once inside the large foyer, Diana murmured, "If you will excuse me, my lord, I believe I shall retire. However, since you are so much recovered, would you join me for dinner this evening? That is, if you do not mind my dining *en déshabillé*. I do not feel up to formal dress."

"It shall be my pleasure, my lady," he replied, his eyes remaining fixed on her face. He was suspicious of her sudden malaise, but she did appear pale. She ascended the stairs as he stared after her, her slender figure graceful and elegant. Did nothing disturb her composure?

"Lady Rossley is ill?" Boswell asked.

"She has the headache." Lord Rossley turned from the view of his wife and looked sharply at his long-time butler. "Does she experience them often?"

"I have never known her to complain of them in the past, my lord."

"Just as I thought. Thank you, Boswell." Damn! The woman was determined to coddle him as if he were Melly. The thought of his child brought chagrin to Lord Rossley. Whatever else his wife did, she had been a good mother to his child. With a sigh, he moved towards the library.

"Dawson is awaiting you abovestairs, my lord."

"With explicit instructions to put me to bed, I'm sure," he said wryly. "I am much recovered, Boswell."

"So we all hope, my lord, but it doesn't do to take chances. The doctor said—"

"I know what the doctor said. I was there." At his butler's stubborn silence, Lord Rossley relented. "All right, Boswell, I'll rest until dinner. Will that satisfy you?"

"Yes, my lord," Boswell said primly, but his smile rewarded his master.

Lord Rossley slowly went up the stairs. In truth, his bed would feel welcome. The outing had exhausted him more than he had expected.

DIANA REMAINED in her room until her maid ascertained that Lord Rossley had not only gone to his bedchamber but also was asleep. Dawson had gladly entered into a conspiracy with the rest of the household to ensure that Lord Rossley did not overexert himself. After his initial meeting with his master's wife, he recognized both the young woman's good intentions towards Lord Rossley and her talent for manoeuvring a sometimes difficult man.

"Tell Dawson his master is joining me for dinner, Cassie, but that I have told him I will dine *en déshabillé*. That way Lord Rossley will not feel compelled to dress in formal attire."

"Yes, my lady. That's a good idea."

The girl slipped away to carry out her mistress's orders and Diana sank into a chair with a sigh. Though Lord Rossley might have been a difficult invalid, the next few weeks were going to be much more complicated.

As an invalid, Lord Rossley had complied with his wife's ordering of his days, albeit reluctantly at times. Now that he was up and about, Diana felt sure he would not be so easily led—particularly when the subject was Hetta Chadwell.

Her fingers trembled as she smoothed a wrinkle from her skirt. Even more complicated would be his intentions in regard to their marriage. Her own thoughts were confused about the man in the next room. She owed Lord Rossley much . . . for her happiness, indeed for her very life. Her care of him in the sickroom had begun as repayment. When had that changed to . . . affection?

CHAPTER FOUR

"MADAM, I WILL NOT countenance this conspiracy!"

Diana looked up from the weekly menus she was contemplating to the seething man in front of her.

"I beg your pardon, Richard. Have the meals not been to your liking?"

Her whimsical response was disregarded. "You know I am not speaking of food. I am referring to the games you and the servants have been playing."

Smiling pleasantly, Diana rose from her desk and moved to the bell-pull before seating herself on the petit-point sofa. With a wave of her hand, she indicated her husband should join her. He looked no less irritated, but he followed her to the sofa.

Boswell entered the morning-room.

"Would you bring us a tea tray, please? I am feeling peckish this morning."

After the door closed behind the butler, Lord Rossley ground out, "That is exactly what I mean! I am sure you ordered tea on my behalf. If I want tea, I will ask for it!"

"I did not know you objected to my taking tea in the mornings, Richard."

"Madam! I will stand for this no longer. Cease and desist!"

"Perhaps if you explained what set you off?" Diana suggested, a small smile on her pleasant features.

"Abbott."

"Ah. I told him I did not believe his plan would work."

"So you did know about it?"

Her husband's complexion remained heightened in colour, his anger not yet appeased. However, Diana seemed unaffected by it. "Yes, of course."

"Well, I'll not have it!" When she made no response, he demanded, "Do you understand me, madam?"

"Of course I do, Richard. You have expressed yourself quite clearly. However, I do not have the heart to tell those who hold you dear that they should no longer care whether you survive or not. It seems so harsh in the face of their love."

Her serenity undisturbed, Diana smiled at Boswell as he entered the room, carrying a well-filled tray. "Cook just took these muffins from the oven, my lady. She thought they might tempt your appetite."

"Wonderful, Boswell. Please thank her for me."

She busied herself pouring two cups of tea, handing one to her husband. Lord Rossley stared first at the cup in his hand and then at the woman beside him.

"I did not mean..." His voice trailed off, frustration evident on his face.

"Really? I thought that was exactly what you meant."

"No," Richard protested. "But I am capable of determining the length of my ride without my groom pretending his animal has thrown a shoe and insisting on our return to the stables.''

"I did warn Abbott that such a ploy would not work on a veteran campaigner like yourself.''

"Thank you for that, at least,'' he said dryly.

Her sunny smile didn't please him. "I'm afraid you must accept some of the blame for this conspiracy, as you call it.''

"Me?''

"Yes, of course. It seems you have the reputation of being a terrible patient, of not taking care of yourself." Diana buttered a hot muffin and placed it on a delicate china saucer before handing it to her husband. Her words were so distracting that he began munching her offering without even being aware of it.

"You do not know that,'' he protested.

With a laugh Diana said, "No, but I have had many people anxious to tell me. Most of your servants have been in your service since you were quite small. And then there are Aunt Margaret and Edward and Robert. They each have many tales of your impatience with illness.''

Rolling his eyes in protest, Richard felt the last of his anger slip away as he studied Diana's elegance. "It is not fair. I have no one to tell tales on you.''

A shadow crossed her face, quickly dispelled. Lightly she said, "No, you must take my word that I am a pattern card of behaviour.''

He frowned. "I did not mean to cause you pain.''

"You did not. But you do understand my difficulty with this conspiracy.'' She shrugged her shoulders ruefully. "While I have not forbidden their efforts, neither have I encouraged the staff to protect you."

"But you yourself have used stratagems to circumvent my wishes."

Diana grinned. "Not your *wishes,* Richard. I hope I have never gone against your wishes."

"Do not mince words with me. You ended our ride in the Park the other day because you thought I was too tired to continue."

"Was I wrong?"

Such a direct question made Lord Rossley shrug and turn away from her. "No," he answered shortly. "But that is a different matter."

Diana sipped her tea, her eyes lowered.

Before Lord Rossley could tax his wife further, Boswell opened the door. "My lord, Mr. White and Sir Robert are below."

"With your permission?" Richard asked Diana, receiving a nod in return. "Send them up, Boswell, and bring more tea."

The two men burst into the room, excitement on their faces. "Was that you in the Park this morning, Richard?" Edward demanded.

"Yes, it was. I didn't see you there."

"I tried to catch up to you, but you were gone before I could break loose from the crowd. I ran into Rob and we decided to follow you home."

Sir Robert slapped his old friend on the back. "I did not know you were recovered enough to sit a horse."

Diana watched the shuttering of Richard's eyes as he turned his left side away from his friends and indicated with his right hand that they be seated. "I am not fully recovered, but the inactivity has been driving me mad.''

Boswell reentered the room with additional offerings, withdrawing as Diana indicated her willingness to serve.

Handing each of the visitors a cup of tea, she sipped her own and made no attempt to join in the conversation.

''Does that mean you will attend the parties now?'' Edward asked. ''Your admirers are awaiting your appearance.''

Richard appeared startled by his friend's words. Before he could ask his meaning, Sir Robert added, ''Never mind, Edward. *We* are anxious for you to join us.''

''Besides, Diana is sadly missed.''

''I have not forbidden Diana to attend social functions,'' Richard snapped. All three men looked at the young woman calmly drinking her tea.

''I have enjoyed the respite,'' Diana said, smiling at her glowering husband. ''But I hoped to persuade Richard to join me tomorrow night at Mrs. Hudspeth's musicale. It will be a small gathering.''

''Sara and Clare wish to attend also. The Italian soprano everyone is talking about is supposed to appear.'' Edward didn't sound enthusiastic. ''And I'm insisting Rob bear me company.''

Sir Robert shuddered. ''Must we? These foreign singers do not appeal to me.''

''No, you prefer the theatre with its Green Room,'' Diana said with arched eyebrows, causing Sir Robert to turn red.

"What do you know of such things?" Richard demanded, his eyes drawn sharply to her.

"Sara told me," Diana explained, undisturbed by Richard's consternation.

Edward groaned as his friend turned to stare at him. "I didn't know she would tell anyone, Richard. Besides, Diana is a married woman, not some innocent, you know."

"Why are you upset?" Robert demanded. "It is my reputation your wife has sullied."

Diana smiled at her husband's dilemma. He could scarcely explain to his friends that his wife was inexperienced. Yet, knowing it himself, he felt her knowledge of the Green Room was inappropriate. She distracted the other two. "I think it is time Rob looked about for a suitable wife. After all, now that Richard has returned safely from the war, the three of you will be together a great deal."

Edward joined in. "You are right, Diana. It is high time for Rob to give up his ramshackle ways and settle down."

"Here now! There is nothing wrong with my life. Marriage is not for me."

Diana smiled gently at one of her favourites. "I don't think it's fair to deny the young ladies of the ton the opportunity to make you happy."

"Young ladies prefer gentlemen who are whole, who are able to dance them round the ballroom," Sir Robert muttered, not meeting Diana's gaze.

An awkward silence fell among them until Diana said calmly, "I do not believe a young woman chooses her husband because he is a good dancer."

"Besides, you will want an heir," Edward added, "and you are not...er...uh..." He paused as his eyes fell on Diana and he remembered her presence. "You—you are not destitute."

Diana rose, hoping she hid her laughter. "If you gentlemen will excuse me, I must return these menus to Mrs. Boswell. Perhaps we shall see you tomorrow evening if I can persuade Richard to accompany me."

Once the door had closed behind her, Edward let out a sigh of relief. "Sorry, Richard. Diana is so comfortable to be around, that I almost forgot myself."

Richard growled an acknowledgement, but his mind dwelt on the unwelcome dilemma of protecting his wife from the sophisticated remarks his friends would never have made before an innocent.

Edward turned to Sir Robert. "As I was saying before good manners forced me to swallow my remark, you have no difficulty in satisfying women off the dance floor. I see no reason for you to shy away from marriage because you cannot waltz."

"There is no hurry," Robert responded, feeling backed into a corner.

"Yes, there is. Now that Richard has returned, I'm sure he and Diana will be setting up their nursery. After all, he has no sons, and Sara and I expect to increase our brood." Edward smiled complacently at his friend, sure he was envious of his domestic bliss.

Fortunately Edward was watching Robert and did not see Richard's startled look.

"Papa, I don't want a baby brother," Melly abruptly said during nursery tea.

Teacups were suspended in mid-air as both adults took in the child's words.

"Melly, you should not—" Diana began hurriedly.

"Why do you say that?" Lord Rossley interrupted, a frown on his face.

The child's chin dropped as she muttered, "Nicholas said I would have a baby brother 'cause you've come home."

"And why wouldn't you want one?" Diana asked quietly before Richard could respond.

Melly abandoned her tea and rushed into Diana's arms. "You're *my* mama! I don't want you to be someone else's mama."

Diana hugged the child tightly to her bosom. "Darling, I will always be your mama—and I will always love you, no matter what."

"Aren't you concerned about me?" Richard demanded, casting a jaundiced eye on the embracing pair.

His tone did not disturb Melly who, with her arms still wrapped tightly about Diana's neck, replied blithely, "You *have to* be my papa, because you are." Her giggles were muffled as she hugged Diana again.

"Thank you. That makes me feel much better," Lord Rossley said wryly.

For such a young child, Melly was very sensitive to others. She slid from Diana's arms to go to her father. "I love you, Papa, and I'm very glad you came home."

He returned her hug. "Thank you, sweet child. I, too, am glad I returned." Setting the little girl from him, he added, "Now finish your tea, or I vow I'll eat your gingerbread man myself."

Melly's squeal of protest ended their discussion. The two adults sat silently, watching the child eat. Diana had been surprised when Richard joined them. But she discovered Melly had planned the family tea. A recent visit to the Whites' household had led to several questions from the child as well as the observation about the expansion of their family.

Once the maid had been summoned, Lord Rossley and his wife descended the stairs to the second floor. As Diana opened the door to her chamber, Lord Rossley said, "Such subjects would be better avoided around the child."

His stiff bearing proclaimed his embarrassment, as did Diana's pink cheeks. "I did not speak on such a subject in front of Melly. She said she heard it from Nicholas."

"And who in God's name is Nicholas?"

"Your godchild, I believe—and Edward's oldest."

"Melly visits Nicholas?" Richard demanded, ignoring his embarrassing memory lapse.

"When I pay a call at Sara's, I frequently take Melly. She loves to play with Nicholas and Sally."

Unable to discover anything to reproach in her words, Richard muttered, "He would not have said such a thing if he hadn't overheard someone else discussing the subject."

Diana stared at him with cool eyes. "I can assure you it was not I." With an elegant sweep of her skirts, she disappeared into her chamber.

"I did not mean—" Richard announced to the closed door. With a shrug, he moved on to his rooms. He knew whom to blame: that blasted Edward with his romantical notions. Unlike himself, Edward still believed in the happy-ever-after of the fairy tales.

THE NEXT MORNING, Diana's duties were again interrupted, but this time by Mrs. Chadwell. Diana greeted her visitor with a warm smile. "Good morning, Hetta. How nice of you to call."

Her good humour was lessened by Mrs. Chadwell's tragic pose. "Is *he* here?"

"If you mean Richard, I believe he is still above-stairs. Come, sit down. I'm sure Boswell will bring us some tea. He is so reliable."

"But if Richard discovers me in his house, he will have those deliciously large footmen remove me at once." She fluttered her lace hanky to her nose.

Diana wasn't sure whether Hetta dreaded or looked forward to such an event. "I hope I may receive guests. This is my home as well as Richard's."

Boswell's entrance with the tea tray decided Mrs. Chadwell. She settled down beside Diana and deliberated over her choice of pastry.

Remaining silent, Diana watched her guest from the corner of her eye. She hadn't spoken to Mrs. Chadwell since that confrontation in the Park.

As if reading her thoughts, the woman said, "I have scarce recovered from the wound Richard dealt me the other day. How cruel he was!"

"Now, Hetta, you must remember how querulous an invalid can be. Besides, both Aunt Margaret and I warned you a reconciliation would take time."

"But I could not help myself!" The lady's expressive face brought a smile to Diana's. "To see him alive before my very eyes when I had been imagining him at death's door! My dear, had it been possible, I would've thrown my arms about his neck!"

Diana couldn't help but imagine Richard's outrage if his mother-in-law had done so. "Hetta, you must be patient."

"Have you spoken to him of me?"

Mrs. Chadwell's eager question filled Diana with remorse. She had intended to plead Hetta's cause with her husband before now, but the two of them were hardly on cosy terms. And how could she deal with others' problems when she could not make any progress with her own?

"Not yet. I . . ."

"But I want to take Melly with me on a picnic! Lady Astley invited us to join her and her two granddaughters on a picnic in the country. Of course, her grandchildren can't hold a candle to Melly as to looks, but they are prettily behaved and will provide her some companionship."

"I'm sure Melly would be delighted to join you, Hetta," Diana agreed, knowing the two little girls to be friends from past excursions.

"Do you think Richard will allow it?"

Diana's lips firmed. "I see no need to consult him. After all, I am Lady Melanie's mama and have had the ordering of her life for more than a year. If I say she may go, then she may."

"You would stand up to Richard?" she asked, awe in her voice. "I vow the man can reduce me to tears with just a look."

"There is no need to be concerned," Diana assured her calmly. She rose and pulled the rope to summon Boswell. When he appeared, she asked that Nanny dress Melly in outdoor wear and bring her to the parlour.

The two women chatted in desultory fashion as they waited for the child's appearance, but Mrs. Chadwell gave a frightened glance at the door each time any noise was heard.

Once grandmother and granddaughter had departed, both in high spirits, Diana sank down on the sofa, limp with relief. For all her apparent coolness, she was relieved to have avoided a confrontation with her husband. He was distant enough as it was.

Diana chided herself for her dissatisfaction. Lord Rossley's coldness was to be expected. She was being too greedy. With an unconscious sigh, she stared ahead gloomily. Greedy or not, she couldn't help but regret the distance between herself and her husband.

Though she knew almost nothing of the stranger who had rescued her that fateful night, while he was away a picture had gradually formed in her mind of a kind, strong man, a man she could rely on, unlike her father who had frequently seemed little more than a child. Between Lady Margaret's memories and those of Richard's friends and the respect shown by his servants, Richard, Lord Rossley, had become in Diana's mind her knight in shining armour, rescuing her from death's door and setting her down in her very own Garden of Eden.

With a gurgle of laughter almost like a sob, Diana thought of the growling bear of a man she now found herself married to. And yet, in spite of her disillusionment, she found herself drawn to him more and more. His love for Melly pleased her—but she believed he fought against it. And he had rejected almost every overture she herself had attempted.

And yesterday, when he had made it clear he thought she hoped to seduce him to produce another child, Diana had been completely humiliated. But after tossing and turning in her bed until the early hours, she had come to terms with her situation.

By the time she finally dropped off to sleep, she had resolved to continue as Melly's mama, to occupy herself with the duties of the household and to leave Lord Rossley strictly alone.

FOR THE FIRST TIME since his return, Lord Rossley did not see his wife at all until the next evening. She had sent word through Dawson that she hoped he would join her at Mrs. Hudspeth's musicale, but she herself had avoided him.

It irritated him when he found himself listening for her footsteps. He had yet to come to terms with life since his return, but an emotional attachment to any woman, particularly his wife, was certainly not in his plans. His first wife had taught him a valuable lesson in showing how perilous such attachments could be.

Dawson helped him into a stark black jacket and the straight-legged pants Brummel had made so popular. He added a snow-white waistcoat in brocade topped by his expertly tied cravat *à l'arbre*.

Quite pleased with himself, even though he had to hold his left arm stiffly to his side, Rossley descended to the parlour, prepared to face Society for the first time in more than a year. Unfortunately, Diana was not yet downstairs. He sat down to rest, though his strength had improved in just the past few days.

The door opened and Diana stood before him. It was the first time he had ever seen her dressed for the evening. The gossamer blue gown revealed a well-shaped bosom and creamy shoulders. Though her lips refused to smile, she still presented an exquisite picture for her husband.

"You are magnificent, my lady," he finally murmured, taking her hand and raising it to his lips.

With a slight curtsy, Diana responded, "Thank you, my lord."

"It is no wonder you have been missed at the social gatherings. They must feel a bright star had disappeared."

"Have you been abroad so long that you have forgotten how beautiful England's young women are?" she asked coolly. "I am scarce noticed when Clare enters the room."

Richard stared down into her eyes, his blue ones serious, as he said, "I cannot imagine such a thing. Anyone would always be aware of your presence." His words surprised even himself, and he dropped her hand and turned away. "Are you ready? We do not want to be late and miss the Italian singer."

Shaken by what he had said, Diana murmured her assent and kept her eyes lowered.

CHAPTER FIVE

WHEN THE ROSSLEYS entered Mrs. Hudspeth's drawing-room, a loud cheer arose from those assembled. Richard, taken by surprise, stared about him. "What is it?"

"They are giving you a hero's welcome," Diana whispered just before their hostess reached them.

"Oh, Lord Rossley, I am so thrilled to be the first hostess to receive our latest hero."

Richard swallowed his irritation and bowed over the woman's hand. After all, it was not her fault that he was being lionized, he supposed. They were soon surrounded by the guests and he found himself greeting old friends and acquaintances.

Diana gradually made her way to the edge of the crowd encircling her husband. She had expected something of the sort when Richard first appeared at an evening party, but she found she didn't care for the mad crush. Discovering Sara sitting patiently to one side, she settled beside her with a grateful sigh.

"It is not easy being the wife of a hero, is it, Diana?" Sara asked with a smile.

"No, it is not. That is why I chose Mrs. Hudspeth's party for our first appearance. At least the number of guests is not too great."

"Yes, that was good planning."

"Is Clare here?"

"Yes, I believe she is on the other side of the crush around Richard. Robert is supposed to meet us here."

Diana laughed. "I wasn't sure he would come. It seems he does not care for foreign singers."

"Edward was pleased that you suggested Robert marry," Sara said as she studied her hands folded neatly in her lap. "Do you have anyone in particular in mind for Robert's wife?"

Diana noted her friend's hesitant manner, but she was not concerned. She knew the cure for Sara's reserve. "Of course I do. Clare."

"Oh!" Sara exclaimed, her face beaming, "I am so relieved. I could not betray Clare's trust, but I did not want you scheming to bring about someone else's marriage to Robert."

"As if I would, silly. It is clear to everyone except Robert that Clare is in love with him."

"Please do not say that in front of Clare. She would be humiliated to know she wears her heart on her sleeve," Sara warned with a frown. "I do not know how else to encourage Robert, though. Clare has done everything except throw herself into his arms."

Before Diana could reply, Lord Rossley, accompanied by Edward, escaped from those around him and arrived at their side. "I think they are about to begin the music...thank God," Richard murmured as he subsided in a chair beside Diana.

"Is being a hero so onerous, my lord?" she asked with a reserved smile.

"It is worse than the fighting. At least in the army you are allowed to protect yourself."

"Richard," Sara whispered, leaning across Diana, "would you save the two chairs beside you? Clare is with us, and Robert promised to join us."

The two missing members of their party both appeared just as the violinist was tuning his instrument. Diana and Sara exchanged satisfied looks as Clare blushed and slid down beside Robert in all her glory. In truth, there was no one there who could compare to her golden beauty. Her delicate but womanly figure, covered in silver tissue, drew all eyes, but her hazel gaze was fixed on only one man. The two women watching were sure he could not ignore such beauty.

Actually, Robert had been aware of Clare's beauty for a number of years. He had first met her as an awkward fourteen-year-old at his friend's wedding. By the time she reached the advanced age of sixteen, he was entranced. But the war beckoned, and many a night on the Continent he had dreamed of returning a hero to claim the golden child he had left behind.

But he had returned as an invalid, not a hero—or so it seemed in his own mind. And he refused to offer damaged goods to such a shining fairy princess. So he had turned his back on her beauty and steeled himself to watch others court her.

Now he smiled briefly at the young woman and gave his reluctant attention to the well-rounded figure of the Italian soprano. He didn't know which was the most tormenting, sitting beside Clare when he knew he must ignore her, or spending an hour listening to that woman screeching at the top of her voice.

By the time their hostess offered refreshments, all three gentlemen were eager to escape their chairs. Offering to bring drinks to their ladies, they excused themselves.

Clare, Sara and Diana chatted in a desultory fashion about the entertainment, their eyes and their thoughts on the three men who were visible in the doorway.

"Who is that gentleman talking to Richard?" Diana asked her friends as a stranger approached Lord Rossley.

"Oh. That's Lord Wyckham. He's with the War Office," Sara said. As Diana frowned, she added, "No doubt he's congratulating Richard on his bravery. The entire Town is enthralled with the tales of his glory."

Diana said nothing but her eyes did not leave her husband.

"Does Richard talk about the war?" Clare asked.

Drawing her eyes reluctantly from the four men, she looked at Clare. "No, he has not. Why?"

"I—I merely wondered. I have asked Robert on several occasions about the time he spent on the Continent, but he does not respond."

"It was a most difficult time, Clare," Sara said softly. "He has spoken some with Edward, but even then he is reluctant to open his budget."

"I hate Napoleon!" the younger sister burst out, tears forming in her expressive hazel eyes as she stared longingly at the dark man leaning against the wall.

"Sister, do not stare. Others will notice," Sara cautioned.

"It just takes time to recover from something as devastating as war," Diana murmured, thinking back to her own personal war. "Now that Richard has returned, Robert will be better, Clare. You'll see."

"Yes, of course," she whispered, her gaze falling to her tightly clenched hands.

When the gentlemen tardily reappeared at their sides with cups of ratafia, the ladies were discussing innocuous topics and accepted their apologies with decorum.

Lord Rossley took his place once more beside his wife, a thoughtful frown on his brow.

"Dare I ask if the evening has become too tiring?" Diana whispered, her concern for Richard's recovery overcoming the reserve their previous arguments had brought about.

A rueful smile accompanied his answer. "Would that I could use that excuse. It is not my stamina that is at fault, but my taste. That woman's caterwauling is beyond bearing."

"Our hostess does not know that your strength has returned, and I, too, have no desire to suffer another hour of her singing."

Richard looked at the twinkle in his wife's grey eyes and squeezed her hand as he picked it up and carried it to his lips, relief filling him. He hated to admit it, but he had missed Diana's friendly smile. "Madam, you are a wife in a million."

He turned to Mr. White. "Edward, we are going to return home. Our hostess will excuse us because of my recent illness. I'm sure you'll be able to give a full report of the second half of the entertainment in the morning.''

''Unfair, Richard! Sara, can you not become violently ill? I have no desire to suffer while the Rossleys escape.''

''I'm afraid it would be too noticeable if we all became ill, my love.''

''Very well, but I do protest your retreat, Richard.''

''What? Richard is leaving?'' Robert demanded, having been distracted by his neighbour.

''Yes, my ill health demands an early night,'' Richard mockingly explained, arching his eyebrows.

''Dam—deuced if it does,'' Robert exclaimed, longingly watching the couple rise. ''Do you need any assistance?''

''No, Robert,'' Diana assured him with a laugh. ''I can attend to my husband.''

''Very well,'' he growled. ''We'll see you in the morning, then, Richard.''

Rossley merely nodded his agreement, and Diana remained silent as they crossed the room. Once they had made their excuses to their hostess and were in their carriage, however, she asked, ''You have an appointment with Robert and Edward in the morning?''

''Yes, I do,'' Richard replied as he leaned back against the wall of the carriage.

When he said nothing else, Diana wondered whether to voice the concern she was feeling. Finally she asked, ''Is that wise? After all, this is your first evening out.''

When his piercing blue eyes raked her face, Diana wished she had held her tongue. His voice was very quiet as he said, "My dear, you have behaved admirably since my return. But I will not tolerate an attempt to rule my life by you or anyone else. Do you understand?"

In the shadowy darkness of the carriage he waited for a response that did not come. Finally he added, "I hope I have not offended you with my plain-speaking."

A cool voice responded. "No, my lord. I daresay I shall remember in the future not to feel concern about your health, or any other matters pertaining to you. My apologies for this evening."

"Diana..." Before he could say more, the carriage door was swung open by their footman and his wife had slipped from the carriage and entered the house.

DIANA STRODE UP AND DOWN her chamber, swishing her skirts as she whirled about. "You knew better!" she berated herself angrily. Only that morning she had set boundaries for herself, and at the first opportunity, she had leapt over them—and received exactly the treatment she should have expected from her husband.

Her pacing halted and she sank down on the bed wearily. Try as she might to remain detached, her concern for the stubborn man next door made it impossible. A lone tear slipped down her cheek. He wounded her so with his cold tones.

With a resolute lifting of her chin, Diana rose and began to undress. She reminded herself to be grateful for all Richard had provided and assist him in his endeavours. Stiffening her features to wipe away the longing, she told herself that above all she must never, never ask for more. If love was not to be hers, she had to be content with what she had. With a sigh, she snuffed out the candle.

RICHARD HAD EVERY intention of behaving amiably the next morning. He knew he had been abrupt with his wife the previous evening. Though he certainly did not intend to reveal his plans to the woman, or to be tied to her apron-strings in any other fashion, she had served him well in his absence. He owed her politeness at the very least.

It took only minutes for his amiability to fly out the window. Rising later than he intended, he had time only for a quick visit to the nursery before descending to the breakfast parlour. However, those few minutes sufficed for Melly to tell him of her excellent adventures with Grandma Hetta at the picnic.

By the time Richard reached the breakfast table, he was steaming more than the pot of tea on the sideboard.

"How dare you!" he burst out as he discovered the villainess buttering a scone.

With her good resolutions in the forefront, Diana remained calm, staring first at her husband, then at the scone, then back to her husband. A small smile played about her lips as she replied, "Do you think a second one too much? Very well, I shall not eat it. But I must confess, I find—"

"Stop it!" Richard roared. "Your lamentable sense of the ridiculous will not spare you, madam. You have deliberately countermanded my orders. I will not have such disobedience in my household."

"Since you have no objection, I believe I *will* eat my scone."

Richard stared at her, stunned. He was a kind man, a considerate employer. But when he lost his temper, he was a formidable opponent, and all in his household trembled in their boots when they heard him roar, from the lowest tweeny to his wife and her mother. But that was no longer the case, Richard suddenly realized. His *first* wife had trembled; *this* wife was fastidiously enjoying her scone. He watched with a sense of amazement as she raised her teacup to her lips without a suggestion of a tremor.

He moved forward and leaned over the table. "Madam, did you hear me?"

"I should think everyone in the household heard you, Richard. Do you always discuss personal issues so openly?" Her look of calm interest reminded him of his mother, the only woman able to withstand his temper, and brought a shiver of inexplicable alarm.

With his jaw clenched, Lord Rossley stared at the wall behind the young woman and muttered, "I will see you in my study at once."

"Would you not prefer to take breakfast first?" Diana asked. "It is so difficult to sustain anger on an empty stomach."

Her words incited him even more. Had she no fear of him? He turned on his heel and marched across the foyer and down the hall to his personal domain.

Diana sighed and took a last sip of her tea. She had hoped to avoid a confrontation for a few more days, but if her guess was accurate, Melly had forestalled that cowardly thought. She stood and followed Lord Rossley down the hall.

When she entered the study, Diana found her husband with his back to the door, resolutely staring up at the painting of his first wife which hung over the fireplace.

The words she would have spoken were swallowed and she waited in silence for him to acknowledge her presence. Many a time in his absence, she had stared up at the woman who had bequeathed Melly to her. There was sorrow that such beauty should now be dust, and just a hint of jealousy that this woman had had her husband's love.

Lost in her thoughts, she jumped slightly when Lord Rossley whirled round.

"Aha! So you do have some fear of me?" Richard asked, pleased.

"You startled me," Diana replied, regaining her composure and seating herself on the gold brocade sofa near the desk.

His lips tightening, Richard prowled in front of the sofa before finally responding. "Madam, I will not have my child consorting with that she-devil. No reasoning of yours will change my mind. All I ask of you is obedience." When there was no response, he stared down at her. "Do you understand me?"

"Your words are quite clear, my lord," Diana said stiffly. "However, I cannot agree with your sentiments."

"I did not ask for your agreement," Richard snapped. "Only your obedience."

"Very well, my lord. I will respond more clearly. I cannot agree with your orders." She drew a deep breath before adding, "I cannot obey."

As the formidable man turned to stare at her, astonishment on his face, Diana hurriedly said, "Please, my lord, I do not mean to displease you, but I disagree with your instructions in this matter."

"You have no choice, madam. I will not allow my daughter to repeat her mother's ways." His gaze returned to the portrait and Diana saw the torment in his eyes.

"Please, Richard, listen to reason. There is no—"

"Reason, madam?" He turned away to return to his pacing. "You know nothing of the pain others can cause, the torture they give the innocent heart."

Diana rose to her feet. "Do you think, my lord," she whispered, "that you pulled me from the Thames because I had a whim to indulge in a swim?"

Her challenge brought him to a halt. He stared at the stern-faced young woman, the softness and humour that marked her countenance gone as they both recalled the events which had led her to the river's edge that night.

Before he could speak, she continued. "I, as well as you, know the damage a selfish person can wreak. Do you believe I would allow the one I love most in this world to become such a person?" She turned from him and he had to move closer to hear her soft words. "Lady Melanie has given meaning to my days and joy to each waking moment. I would never do anything to cause her harm.''

"Perhaps not intentionally, but—"

"No!" She spun round sharply. "I am not an empty-headed young girl, my lord. I love Melly, but I also know the duties of a parent." She bowed her head and muttered, "My father taught me by his neglect."

Richard made a movement towards the slender figure, but stopped himself. "I believe you love Melly, but her grandmother—that woman is as much to blame for her daughter's behaviour as the poor girl was herself."

"I would not argue that, my lord," Diana said, her head coming up. "But if you and I have learned from the past, do you deny that privilege to Hetta?" She raised her head when Richard would have spoken. "I know she does not show any change. She will always appear as empty-headed as ever, concentrating only on frivolous and trivial things. But she lost her greatest treasure, your wife, and she feels the pain of it within, just as you do."

"I do not grieve for my wife! She means nothing to me now! I never think of—" He stopped at the look of pity on Diana's face.

"I only allow Melly to accompany Hetta when I approve of the outing and the company she will keep. When Hetta and I first met, and she asked to take Melly about, I explained the trust you had placed in me. She agreed to meet any requirements I imposed if she were allowed to share in her granddaughter's life. She has not failed me, sir, and I do not believe she ever will."

"You have more faith than I, madam," Richard muttered, not meeting his wife's eyes.

"You had enough faith to entrust your beloved child to me once. Can you not continue that trust?" The gentleness had returned to her voice and Richard looked at her to discover a smile curving her soft lips.

He stepped forward, stretching out a hand, whether to caress or reprimand, Diana did not know, when there was a knock on the door.

Boswell followed his knock. "Mr. White and Sir Robert are below, my lord."

"I'll be down directly." After the door closed behind the butler, Lord Rossley looked at Diana. "My dear, forgive my temper. I do not like the continued association with that woman, but...but you have served me well this past year. If you believe Melly will come to no harm, I will allow you to regulate her outings unless I see reason to disagree." Before she could respond, Richard left the room.

Diana sank back to the sofa. "I have served him well," she repeated. She smiled ruefully. He thought of her as no more than a superior servant. At least she was superior, Diana mused, the slight smile disappearing. And let that be a warning to her unspoken hopes of a true family, a true bond between that man and herself.

With a sigh, Diana returned to her morning duties, thoughts of Richard heavy on her heart.

"I DID NOT SAY you were ill-mannered," Edward protested as Richard entered the parlour where the two men were awaiting him.

"You might as well have."

"Here now, what is the matter?" Richard enquired as he entered the room.

Rob grunted at the interruption and then turned his back on his two friends. Richard looked at Edward for an explanation.

"I was just pointing out to Rob that his behaviour wounded Clare last evening."

"Did something happen after our departure?"

"Yes. That blasted soprano continued singing to an unconscionable hour," Robert growled.

Edward sent him an exasperated look. "It is not important. But I do not understand why Robert avoids Clare so much. She has begun to notice and is hurt by his behaviour."

"She should not be spending her time with a worn-out soldier. She is young and . . . and the most beautiful angel ever to grace the London scene. There are many young men anxious to share her every waking moment. My presence has no bearing on her life."

His two best friends stared at him with brows drawn together and concerned looks on their faces. He threw his hands up in exasperation and turned his back. "What are you staring at?"

Richard walked over to clap his right hand on Robert's shoulder. "I did not realize you were—"

"What?" Robert barked, wheeling round to dare Richard with his eyes to speak.

Richard fell back, recognizing pain he understood all too well. Edward, however, was not as willing to give in to his friend's feelings.

"If Richard will not say it, I will. You are in love with the chit. What is so shameful about that? And how do you expect to win her heart if you constantly throw her into other men's arms?"

Robert stared at his friend. "Now you have understood, Edward. I have no intention of winning her heart. Would you have that angel trapped by half a man?"

"Oh, you chuckle-head! You never thought of yourself as half a man when you called on Mistress Nell the other evening." As Rob turned red, Edward added slyly, "And I'll vow Mistress Nell didn't, either, when you left at dawn."

Richard stepped between an enraged Robert and Edward, fearing they would come to fisticuffs. "Enough, Edward. You must not interfere in Rob's private matters."

"Thank you," Sir Robert muttered.

"Now, we must be about our business." Richard waved his two friends towards the door. "Lord Wyckham is expecting us to discover names of anyone with recent inexplicable wealth, or someone who might have ties to France. He believes the head of the operation to be a member of Society."

"Where shall we begin?" Edward asked, his friend's behaviour all but forgotten. "I know nothing of skulduggery."

"I thought we might start at Watier's. There are always members there eager to discuss politics."

"I am still not sure talk will accomplish the deed," Rob added, a frown on his face. "I would do more than simply provide him with names of those suspected of supplying Boney.''

''He has his own men to investigate any names we give him, Rob, but they can't move about in Society as we can. Besides, Sara doesn't like my being away.''

''And we are not fit for much else.'' Richard said bitterly. ''I cannot even drive a carriage with only one good arm.''

His friend's complaint brought to Rob's ear an echo of his earlier one. Realizing the fruitlessness of their bitterness, he grinned at his friend. ''And I cannot waltz. But together we shall be a whole man, my friend, and Edward will guide this slightly damaged pair. We shall ever serve our King and country.''

The three men linked arms and strode towards the front door, which was quickly opened by a footman.

Diana, standing on the landing, saw only their backs, but their words disturbed her. Richard had already served his King and country and been injured in return. She did not want him risking anything else. What were they up to?

CHAPTER SIX

FOR THE NEXT several days, Diana watched her husband's comings and goings from a distance. The weariness on his face when he returned from his daily outings almost moved her to protest, but the memory of his coldness bade her remain silent. When she came upon him rubbing his injured arm as if it ached unbearably, she sat down and wrote a note to the doctor, asking him to call on her.

"Lady Rossley, how may I be of service?" Doctor Brownell asked, his eyes smiling as well as his lips.

"Doctor, I know you are a busy man, but my husband has begun going out every day. I believe his arm is paining him, but he becomes angry if I suggest he rest. I wondered if perhaps you could pretend to have dropped in to verify his progress?" Diana waited hopefully while the small man thought about her suggestion.

"Yes, of course, my lady. I would be willing to pretend my arrival here is of my own initiation," he agreed with a smile. "I should have come, actually, but the Prince Regent has had several complaints of late that made it necessary for my strict attendance on him."

"Of course. I appreciate your cooperation. He generally arrives home in about half an hour. Boswell will bring us a tea tray while we wait," Diana said, filled with relief.

While they drank their tea, Doctor Brownell asked several questions regarding his patient's activities, but he received unsatisfactory answers from Lady Rossley. Though he eyed her sharply when she answered in a roundabout way, he said nothing.

Almost like clockwork, Lord Rossley arrived home at his usual time. Boswell, well primed by his mistress, told him Doctor Brownell had called and was awaiting him in the parlour.

With a grimace, Lord Rossley entered the room to discover his wife serving tea with great social grace, which boded well for the request he intended to make as soon as they were alone.

"Good afternoon, Doctor," he said heartily, wishing his arm were not throbbing so. "Have you no sick patients to visit?"

Diana dropped her eyes, afraid her duplicity would show in them, and poured a fresh cup of tea for her husband.

"Aye, my lord. I decided to plump up my fees by calling on old patients. You have no objection, do you?" The man's laughter put Lord Rossley at his ease.

"Of course not. I'd as soon pay you as anyone. Has my wife been entertaining you?" Richard asked, he eyes having noted Diana's avoidance of him.

"Charmingly so. You are a fortunate man, my lord, to have such a lady grace your home."

"So many have told me."

Diana did look up at the note of dryness in his voice, but she quickly lowered her gaze once more when it encountered his bright blue one.

The doctor frowned but gave a short laugh, unsure of his patient's meaning. "Well, in truth, my lord, I thought I might just take a look at that arm. Mustn't let anyone think you cured yourself, you know. Would spoil my reputation."

"'Tis not necessary, Doctor. I go along very well," Richard averred, unconsciously holding his left arm with his right hand.

"I'm sure 'tis not, my lord, but just to satisfy an old man's curiosity, may I examine it?"

Without rudeness, refusal was impossible. Richard looked first at the doctor and then at his wife, who carefully kept her eyes from his. Finally, he said, "I suppose it could do no harm. Shall we retire to my bedchamber?"

Diana carefully schooled her features to show no relief until after the two men had left the room. She only hoped the doctor would realize just how much Richard was rushing his convalescence. And for what reason? She pondered once more what the three men could be doing "for their country." Tempted as she was to do so, she had not yet questioned Sara and Clare to discover if they had any idea. Sara was increasing, though it was early days just yet, and Diana did not want to worry her. And Clare was already upset because Robert continued to avoid her. She would know nothing.

When Doctor Brownell returned to the parlour, Lady Rossley's fearful look as she waited for his verdict supplied the answer to one of his questions.

"My lady, your husband is quite well. He has been going about a little too much of late, but I have counselled him about straining his physical resources, and he has agreed to slow his activities for a few days.

"And his arm?"

"Aye, his arm. Well, now, I warned you there would be no miracles, did I not?" He frowned as he added, "I believe there is some progress, but it is very slight. The muscles are responding, but the arm is virtually useless at the moment."

"And in the future?" Diana asked softly. It mattered not to her, but she knew Richard would hate to be crippled.

"Who is to say? Medicine is not an exact science, my lady. There is much we have not learned about the body... and the mind. I, for one, believe there is a connection between the two. We must be patient and await developments."

With a sigh, Diana smiled at the man and held out her hand, much to his surprise. "Thank you, Doctor Brownell. You have assisted me greatly."

"Feel free to call on me at any time. I might add," the doctor said with a twinkle in his eye, "that I have assisted quite a number of ladies in their confinements."

Diana's face froze and her eyes filled.

"My lady, I did not intend to offend," Doctor Brownell hurriedly said, his eyes studying her reaction.

"No, no, of course no," she muttered, looking away. "I—I shall keep that in mind."

Now that another of his questions had been answered, Doctor Brownell added softly, "My lady, there is nothing to keep your husband from...from any of his husbandly duties."

Diana's cheeks flamed but she reminded herself she was no schoolroom miss. Nor would she allow anyone to pry into such private matters, even the good doctor. "Thank you, Doctor. You have greatly relieved my mind."

Since she rose to her feet and waited, the doctor had no choice but to stand also. "I am always at your service," he said with a bow and left the room.

Diana had not fully recovered from the doctor's words when Lord Rossley entered the parlour. His words came as no surprise after his piercing looks earlier. "Did you send for the doctor, madam?"

Diana looked up at the man towering over her and did not bother to lie. "Yes, of course I did. Forgive me for having concern for your health, my lord. I'll try to restrain such impulses in the future."

Left with nothing to say, Richard could only frown at his wife. Finally, he ground out, "Thank you."

Feeling relieved that she had forestalled a lecture, Diana smiled up at him. "For having concern or for promising to have less concern in the future?"

The grey eyes twinkling up at him dissolved Richard's anger. With a rueful smile, he said, "Perhaps a little of both, madam."

As she responded to his unthawing, Diana's smile widened. Alarmed by such warmth, Richard backed away. "But there will be no need for the doctor in the future. I am recovering admirably."

"If you do not try to do so at too rapid a pace," Diana muttered, unhappy that he had rejected her friendship.

"I am not a child, madam," Richard snapped.

"No, you are not, but if you do not stop using that horrid appellation every time you address me, I vow I shall . . . shall box your ears!"

He stared at her mutely.

With a sigh, Diana said, "I apologize for my anger, Richard, but my name is Diana, not 'madam.' If you cannot bring yourself to address me so . . . so intimately, then you may call me Lady Rossley, or my lady, or even my wife. But at least do not call me madam, as you would a stranger on the street, or a fishmonger's wife when you are shopping."

"My apologies, my lady," Richard said stiffly.

With a disgusted look on her face, Diana rose and moved towards the door.

"Where are you going?" Richard demanded.

"To dress for dinner," she answered, without turning round.

"Stay but a moment. I—I have something to ask of you."

Sudden fear filled Diana. Had he decided he did not want to continue with her as his wife? Divorce was not common, but it did occur occasionally. Slowly, she turned to face him.

"Yes, my lord?"

"I wondered if you would mind hosting a party?"

Relief flooded Diana at such a mundane request. "I would be delighted to do so. I have been graciously received among the ton and it would be delightful to reciprocate for the many functions I have attended."

"I had more in mind a small entertainment, just dinner and—and cards, perhaps."

"I did not know you were a card player, my lord."

Richard's cheeks reddened. "It is an accepted entertainment, that's all."

"I see. And just whom did you wish to invite to this party?"

Without hesitation, Richard reached into an inner pocket and retrieved a list of names he, Edward and Robert had prepared. "Here are those I would have included."

Diana stared at him, frowning. Obviously this was not a spur-of-the-moment notion. She looked at the list. "But, Richard, these people are . . . are older, and most of them are gentlemen. You cannot have a dinner party almost entirely made up of gentlemen." *And mostly dullards,* she added silently.

"Well, of course, we would include their wives. Wouldn't that give us sufficient number?"

"All these people are your friends?"

"Well, perhaps not close friends, but I know them all. And Edward and Robert have acquaintances among them." He looked uncomfortable under her questioning.

"Of course I will be the hostess for the party. When would you like to have it?"

"As soon as possible."

"I must consult my calendar, but I believe next month—"

"No! It must be at once."

Diana started at him. "But Richard—"

"At once, Diana," he said firmly, self-consciously adding her name to turn her up sweet.

One eyebrow rose as a cool smile appeared on her lips. "Nicely said, my lord," she commented, before adding. "I shall try to arrange the party within the week, but I had best confer with Sara, if you do not mind."

"She will agree to whatever date you select."

Stranger and stranger. "How do you know that?"

"Edward has assured me he and Sara would be delighted to attend."

It was clear to Diana that this was not an ordinary social gathering, but it was also clear that Richard had no intention of confiding in her. She studied the list once more to see if there were any ladies invited in whom he might have an unusual interest. However, there were none to raise suspicions. "Very well. I shall select several dates and visit with Sara first thing in the morning to confirm them. Then I shall send out cards. Will that suffice?"

"That will do nicely," he agreed with relief.

"And will there be any objection if we add a few names to increase the conviviality of the evening?"

"Yes, of course, as long as it remains a small gathering, where there will be conversation."

"HE ACTUALLY SAID THAT?" Sara asked.

"Yes. Can you think of any entertainment this Season where there has been *no* conversation? Why, even at a musicale, there is plenty of opportunity for chit-chat."

Sara laughed. "Diana, if there were not, the Season would be unbearably boring, for it is the gossip that holds everyone's interest."

"Sara, do you know what they are up to?" Diana suddenly asked, a frown on her brow.

"What are you talking about?" her friend asked, confused.

"Last week, they left the house, the three of them, arms linked and talking about serving their King and country. Since then, Richard has been out and about in Society, even though he does not care for such things. Now, he suddenly requests a party and provides me with an impossible guest list, already prepared, demanding that it take place immediately."

"You are right, Diana. The three of them have been going about a great deal these past few days. I—I have missed Edward's presence. But I did not want to complain because I attributed their excitement to Richard's return and recovery."

"I think it is something other than that. I am afraid—" Diana paused, chewing her lip, debating whether to share her thoughts with her friend.

"Go on, Diana. What is it?"

"You do not suppose they could be spying for the government, do you?" Diana asked in a rush.

Sara's cheeks paled and Diana wished she had not spoken. "Please, Sara, I am surely wrong. You must disregard my words."

"Oh, Diana, I am afraid you are right. Edward has felt so bad that he did not go to serve his country when his friends did. But we already had Nicholas, and Sally was on the way. I could not have managed on my own." She buried her face in her hands, tears washing her cheeks. "I am afraid he has resented us because of that."

Diana moved to the sofa beside her friend and put her arms about her. "Nonsense, Sara. Edward loves you all dearly. I have never seen a prouder papa than Edward."

With a watery chuckle, Sara said, "He does enjoy the children."

"Without a doubt. And with a third on the way, I'm sure Edward would never—"

"I have not told him."

"What? But I thought . . . you said you were going to tell him last week."

"Yes, and I intended to do so, but he went out with Robert and Richard and did not return until the wee hours of the morning and—and I was miffed."

"Oh. Well, you must tell him at once." Diana felt sure Edward would never enter into any dangerous activities with another child on the way. And if Edward withdrew, perhaps the other two would rethink their behaviour.

"I cannot," Sara wailed, burying her face against Diana's shoulder.

"What is the matter?" Clare demanded as she entered the parlour, throwing off her cape to reveal a stylish peach muslin gown.

Having been sworn to secrecy about the baby, and not wanting to reveal her fears to anyone else and cause more problems, Diana stared mutely at her friend.

Sara, however, had no such reservations. Mopping her tears with her palm, she said, "I am *enceinte* and Edward does not know. And Diana thinks the three of them may be engaged in some nefarious activity, like...like spying," she cried, the tears wetting her cheeks again.

"The three of them? Surely you don't mean Robert? But he mustn't! His leg! He might reinjure himself or—or even be killed!"

Before Diana knew it, both her friends were upset and she felt the veriest beast for having said anything. "Please, I am probably wrong. Perhaps it was just a jest."

"What? You must explain yourself," Clare pleaded, regaining control of her emotions.

Diana explained to Clare her concern over her husband's behaviour—as well as that of his friends—and Clare thought the whole business peculiar as well.

"Sara must tell Edward that she is with child, and he will withdraw from any dangerous activities. And if he withdraws, perhaps the other two will also do so."

Clare's assessment closely aligned with Diana's and both women turned to the third.

"Do you not see? That is the one thing I cannot do!" Sara exclaimed.

"But why?" Clare demanded. "Edward wants more children. He will be delighted to add to his brood."

"Of course he would have been delighted, a month ago. But now, when he feels he is finally able to serve his country, just as his friends have done, I cannot take that away from him. That is precisely what happened the last time Richard and Robert volunteered their services." Sara pleaded with her eyes as well as her words for the others' understanding.

"Oh, dear," Diana muttered. "I do understand, but—"

"I do not! I refuse to let Robert face any danger if I can prevent it." Clare's stubborn expression almost brought a smile to her sister's face.

"Oh, Clare, I wish I could think that also, but when you have been married for a while, you come to understand the way a man thinks a little better."

"*I* am willing to be married. It is Robert who is making it impossible," Clare said with a hiccup which sounded more like a sob.

"And that is something else we must deal with," Diana said before turning her attention back to the matter at hand. "Now, my speculations may not be accurate. We must keep that in mind. But if we cannot persuade them to give up whatever they are doing, then we must do our best to protect them."

"I will volunteer to be constantly in Robert's company to protect him," Clare offered with great daring.

"Edward will send you back to the country to live with Mama if you do not have a care," Sara assured her. "But Diana is right. We must do what we can to assist them."

"I did not say to assist them, Sara. I said to protect them," Diana inserted, exasperated.

"Yes, of course, we must do both. First, we must discover what they are about. Let's have a look at the guest list once more, Diana."

Pulling out the much-studied list, the ladies scrutinized it again, but to no avail.

"Richard truly wants to invite these people? There are even some from the merchant class included." Clare stared at Diana as if she might have fabricated the list herself.

"I assure you, the list came from Richard. And I suspect it was written with Edward and Robert's assistance. The merchants are quite warm in the pocket. One of them, Sir Toby Bartholomew, was knighted by Prinny just last year for his efforts in the war."

"And the others? Do they have anything to do with supplying the Army on the Continent?" Sara asked.

Diana stared at her friend admiringly. "Of course! Why did I not think of that?" She turned back to the list. "Yes, several of them are involved in sales to the Army. But what of Sir John Gillian? He is against the war. Why would he be on the list?"

The two others frowned in thought but had no answers.

"So, what shall we do?" Clare finally asked.

"I must give the party. I gave my word to Richard. But he did agree to my adding to the guest list. Will you help me choose a few other guests to help enliven the affair?"

The three women put their heads together for half an hour and added another ten names to the list, evening out the number of men and women and also adding those who would carry the conversation.

"And we must all three be on the alert. Surely we can discover what they are doing before too long," Sara added. "After all, I am almost two months along now. It will not be long before Edward will discover my secret without any assistance from me."

"True. But there is one other concern I must put on our list," Diana added, giving Clare a sly look. "I think we should all work together to bring about Robert's marriage... to Clare," she added, knowing she should not tease her friend but finding it irresistible.

Clare's cheeks flamed but she nodded vigorously. "I willingly accept your help," she assured Diana. "I have done everything myself to let him know that I— I care, but he has not responded. Perhaps he truly does not care about me."

"Do not be ridiculous," Diana assured her. "I have seen him look at you when you are in the company of other men. I believe he would murder them cheerfully if Society did not frown on such behaviour."

"But I do not wish to be with other men. I have no choice when he refuses my company, however."

"Robert feels he is not good enough for you because he cannot waltz," Diana said quietly.

Clare stared at her, shock on her face.

"You did not know?"

"Of course I did not know! How could he think such an absurd thing?"

"I think Diana is right," Sara added. "I believe he truly cares for you, and that is the only thing which holds him back."

"But it cannot be! He is a hero! He was wounded fighting for King and country! How could he think I would think any less of him for his wound? If anything, I love him more."

"Perhaps you should tell him so," Diana suggested.

"No, she could not be that forward," Sara assured her friend, but Diana was not convinced of that as she stared at Clare.

"And it might not serve. He would consider your words to be those of a young woman who does not know what is best for her. He does not think himself suitable for you."

"What shall I do?" Clare pleaded. "There must be something I can do to persuade him that he is the only man who can make me happy."

With her own difficulties at home to solve, Diana had nothing to offer Clare as a solution. Sara, also, had no suggestions.

"We shall find something," Sara assured her sister, hugging her. "You must wipe that misery from your face."

"If we all three work at placing you in Robert's company, he cannot possibly escape. And perhaps his feelings for you will overcome his ridiculous pride," Diana suggested. "I shall be sure you are seated next to Robert at our dinner."

"And you must wear that silver gauze you bought last week," Sara added. "It was frightfully expensive, but no man could resist you in that gown."

"Then stay away from Richard," Diana teased. Yet it was true that in her heart she feared any of the beautiful women of the ton. She could not compare to such beauties.

Clare gave her friends a wobbly smile. "I shall wear my silver gown and I shall set next to Robert, but I am not sure it will affect him. He has a heart made of stone."

"Never fear, my dear sister," Sara said, "the three of us are going to work as a trio, just as our difficult men do, and success will be ours. You may be sure of it!"

CHAPTER SEVEN

DIANA SHOWED NO SURPRISE when her husband
joined her that evening as she prepared to depart for
the Sheffields' ball, even though he had not said he
would attend. However, she resolved to keep a close
eye on his activities. It was his first large affair since
his return. Fortunately, Sara and Clare would also be
there.

"Is Robert going to be present this evening?" she
asked as they entered their carriage.

"Yes, he is," Richard responded absent-mindedly,
his eyes studying his wife's pleasing appearance.
"Why do you ask?"

"Oh, no reason. I just knew Sara and Edward
would be in attendance," Diana said, looking out the
window of the carriage after she was seated.

Richard frowned. In spite of himself, he was coming to know his wife. When she refused to meet his
eyes, she had something to hide. "You have a matter
to discuss with Robert?" he asked again, carefully
watching as she smoothed the lavender silk of her
skirt.

"No, of course not."

Richard gave up his questioning, but he resolved to
keep a close eye on his wife during the evening. He had

been cuckolded by his first wife, to the amusement of the ton; he would not be so careless a second time. His lips firmed in determination even as the carriage rocked along the London streets.

"Have you chosen a date for our party?" Richard asked, remembering Diana's promise to consult Sara.

"Oh, yes, I forgot to tell you. I wrote up the invitations this afternoon and sent them out. We decided on the seventeenth, Thursday evening. Is that satisfactory?"

"That's perfect. It's only four days away. Can you be ready then? I want everything to go well." His intensity intrigued his wife.

"Is there any particular reason for this party?"

Unconsciously aping his wife, Richard refused to meet her eyes. "No, of course not," he assured her, adjusting his cuffs. "It is simply my first attempt at entertaining in a long time and I would like everything to go well."

Although she was unconvinced, Diana pretended to accept his statement at face value. "I will ensure the evening will be successful."

"Good. I hope you enjoy entertaining because I propose to have many more such evenings," Richard said, chancing a quick look at Diana's face.

"I have no objection, though I thought you intended to retire to the country soon because you had no use for Town life."

"Nonsense. I had forgot how charming Society can be," Richard said without expression. "I'm sure you find it so."

Looking out the window once more, Diana murmured, "Yes, charming." Nothing else was said until they arrived at the Sheffields' house.

Upon their entry, Richard was lionized, just as he had been at the musicale. Diana slipped away from the crowd to discover Sara and Edward nearby. She joined them.

"What a sad crush," she complained to her friend.

"Yes. Mrs. Sheffield will be thrilled. I did not know Richard was venturing out to such entertainment," Sara said.

"He has refused until this evening. Then suddenly he appeared downstairs ready to accompany me. Oh, thank you, Edward," Diana said as he handed her a cup of punch.

"Now that Diana is here to chat with you, my dear, I believe I'll just stroll about." Edward smiled at his wife, but even Diana noted his nervousness.

"Of course, darling. I'll be fine. Enjoy yourself." Once her husband left her side, Sara whispered to Diana, "See? That is not like Edward. He acted as if he could not wait to leave me."

"Sara, I'll not believe Edward no longer loves you. Why, your marriage has been the toast of the ton. It must be that he is doing whatever we think they are doing. We just must discover what it *is* they are doing." After a pause, Diana gurgled, saying, "Good heavens, I sound like Hetta Chadwell."

The laughter relieved Sara's tension. "You are right, Diana. I know Edward still loves me. But I wish I knew what they are about."

"So do I. Where is Clare?"

"Strolling about the room on Leon Brewster's arm. And that is another thing. Edward is so protective of Clare's reputation. But he had no complaint about Mr. Brewster, and yet he knows the man is a fortune-hunter. It's as if he couldn't be bothered."

"Clare will be safe enough in the ballroom, and she knows better than to retire with such a man. Robert is supposed to be in attendance."

That *non sequitur* made complete sense to Sara. But it also took her by surprise. "Here? But Robert never attends balls."

"So we thought. I think it would behove us to keep a close eye on those three tonight." She fell silent as Richard discovered her and came across the room.

"I thought I would never be free," he complained.

Diana was tempted to ask him about the charm of Society, but felt it would be unfair to do so in front of Sara. "They only wish to salute you as their hero."

"I can only hope some other soldier will take my place soon." With a quick scan of the ballroom, Richard asked, "Where is Edward, Sara?"

"I believe he said he would stroll about the room," Sara replied calmly, sipping her punch.

"Ah. I shall see if I can discover him if you ladies will excuse me," Richard said even as he turned away.

"Well, now we have both been officially abandoned," Diana said. The two women stood there watching Richard melt into the crowd. After a few minutes of conversation, Diana spied Robert coming through the receiving line. "There is Robert. Were I a man, I would make a bet on his abandoning us also."

Sara shook her head. "I would not take the bet. Even without Clare to scare him away, I feel sure he will follow his two friends."

Robert approached them warily. "Good evening, ladies. Have you seen—"

"They are strolling about the room," Diana said in exasperation. "And yes, we will excuse you to go and seek them out."

"Is anything wrong?" Robert asked.

"Oh, no, we prefer to be abandoned in the middle of a ball," Sara said. "After all, it is the fashion."

"I would offer to keep you company but—" Robert began, only to be interrupted by Clare.

"Why, Sir Robert, I did not know you would be in attendance. May I present Mr. Brewster?"

Robert scowled at the fop escorting Clare. "Evening, Brewster. If you'll excuse Miss Seaton, I believe this dance is promised to me."

The orchestra had only begun tuning their instruments and Mr. Brewster seemed reluctant to depart, but Clare smiled warmly at him. "Thank you for escorting me, sir."

Since he had no option, the man bowed and departed.

"What are you doing in that man's company?" Robert demanded angrily.

"Because he asked me," Clare said coolly. "Would you care to escort me, since it seems I *promised* this dance to you?" Dressed in a pale blue muslin trimmed with a delicate lace, Clare drew herself up and stared down her nose in a most regal fashion.

Robert realized he had trapped himself and accepted it with grace. "It is my greatest desire, my dear." He extended his arm and Clare placed delicate fingers upon it. The two strolled away without a thought for the two women left behind.

"Well! I do believe my little sister is growing up."

"Yes, she carried it off well, didn't she?" Diana asked. "I have never seen Robert so neatly manoeuvred."

"What do we do now?" Sara asked.

Diana gave her friend a determined smile. "I believe we should seek out other companions, since our husbands have abandoned us. There is Lord Anthony and Mr. Thomas. Let's see if I can draw them over."

Following Diana's successful bid, she and Sara were led out onto the floor for the first dance. Turning from a heated conversation about England's involvement in the war, Richard saw his wife throw back her head and laugh at something Lord Anthony said. A frown settled on his brow. She had never laughed like that in his presence.

"What is it, Richard?" Edward asked, noticing his distraction.

"My wife is dancing with Lord Anthony."

Edward turned round and looked at the formation on the dance floor. "He is a suitable partner. There is no—Sara! Sara is dancing with Mr. Thomas."

"But he is most suitable, Edward," Richard mocked. "What is the difficulty?"

"Sara is...is a married woman."

"So is Diana. They have danced with others this past year, haven't they?"

"Yes, but Sara always asked my permission first. She danced with my particular friends. Not with one of the most eligible bachelors of the ton." Edward made a movement towards his wife.

"No, Edward. You must not go out on the dance floor. That would cause a scene. We shall meet them when they come off the floor."

Distracted from their set task, the two men wandered closer to the dancers to await their wives. They were joined there by Sir Robert and Clare.

"We did not know you had arrived," Richard said to Sir Robert.

"I did not have an opportunity to join you. Clare needed rescuing," Robert said, glaring at Edward.

Before a bewildered Edward could respond, Clare said, "I apologize for interrupting your evening, Sir Robert. I can assure you I will not bother you any more."

Robert clamped his hand on Clare's arm as she turned to leave. "Do you want to be considered fast? Your chaperon is out on the dance floor. You cannot wander off alone."

"I shall do whatever—" Clare whispered in agitation.

The arrival of the two awaited women brought their argument to a halt. The charming smiles on their faces froze somewhat when they became aware of their reception committee. After introductions were made between their escorts and the others, the two gentlemen who had been their dance partners took themselves off at once.

"Thank you very much," Diana said softly to her husband. "I'm sure those two gentlemen will never dance with us again after your cordial reception."

"Good," Richard murmured, looking away from his wife's sharp stare.

"Sara, I believe you forgot your duties. You are supposed to be Clare's chaperon," Edward reminded his wife.

With her eyebrows raised, Sara only said, "I left her in Robert's care. I thought he would entertain her until my return."

Since Clare was still standing beside Robert, albeit by force, Edward was left with nothing to say. Sara, however, did not like being reprimanded in public and said sweetly, "Did you not want to stroll about the room, my dear? Please feel free to do so. I shall manage to find companions."

Edward White had been married for eight years. He knew when he had displeased his wife. With an apologetic look at his friends, he muttered, "I believe I feel like dancing instead, Sara. Will you accompany me?"

"Why, yes, my love, I'd be delighted to join you." She extended her hand and preceded him to the floor where the orchestra was beginning a waltz.

"Do not be concerned, Clare. I will be glad to chaperon you until their dance is completed," Diana said, knowing her own husband would not come so easily to heel.

"That will not be necessary, Diana. Robert is going to waltz with me." The challenge in the young beauty's eyes was there for all to see.

"I do not—I cannot waltz, Clare. You know that."
Robert's face reddened in anger.

"I believe you can. We shall remain on the fringes
of the crowd, and if you grow tired, we shall stop. But
you have not tried to waltz since you returned."

"She is right, Robert. You will perform admirably," Diana said with a loving smile, knowing Robert's limp had lessened as his injured limb gained
strength.

As the couple moved out onto the dance floor, ap-
prehension visible in Robert's face, Richard kept his
eyes on his wife. He had seen Diana's smile as she
prodded Robert into accompanying Clare. "That was
a terrible thing to do to Robert. If he makes a fool of
himself, he will never forgive you or Clare," he said
harshly.

Diana turned her attention from the couple to stare
at her husband. "Am I to be the only one left without
a partner?" Her challenge shocked her husband.

"You know I cannot lift my left arm, my lady," he
whispered tightly.

"But I can hold it for you and no one will ever
know."

He stared into her gentle grey eyes and found no
malice there. With a formal bow, he led her to the edge
of the floor.

Inconspicuously, Diana took his left hand and lifted
it in the proper fashion as his right encircled her waist
and they swung round the room.

Richard knew the weight of his arm was a strain to
his slender wife. Halfway through the dance, he swung

her towards the edge of the floor. "Damn it! Let's bring this farce to an end."

"You won your wounds honourably, my lord. Will you be a coward now?" Diana's words were cool, but the warmth in her eyes encouraged him.

"It is too much for you," he protested, moving more slowly but still dancing.

"I am enjoying our dance, my lord," Diana assured him. After another long look, Richard swung her round and continued dancing, and Diana breathed a sigh of relief.

They finished the waltz in silence. When the music ended, Richard led her from the floor, anxious to escape. At the edge, they were met by a brazen young matron, set on being the most popular female at the ball.

"Lord Rossley, I did not know you could dance. I hope I may be included as a partner?" She battered her eyelashes at the horror-stricken man.

"I'm afraid that's impossible," Diana said, stepping between the two. "My husband's doctor has limited him to only a few dances, and I insist he give them to me."

"Don't you think you should share? After all, Lord Rossley is a hero and everyone wants to see him," the lady argued, her eyes sparkling.

Without batting an eye, Diana smiled and said, "Perhaps when he is more fully recovered." She slipped her arm inside Lord Rossley's and, without waiting for a response, drew Richard over to the others in their party.

Robert and Clare were arguing about his dancing, while Sara and Edward tried to intervene. Richard, still shaken by the thought of having to dance with others, stared at them without speaking. Diana, however, did not remain silent.

"What is wrong, Robert? You danced very well. Perhaps now you will not hesitate to join us in the evenings."

"Really, Diana, you should not interfere," Richard protested, drawn to speak by his wife's words.

"I think she speaks the truth," Clare asserted, her chin raised as she stared at Robert. "I would rather waltz with you than any other man. You must not hide yourself away." Her boldness caused her sister to gasp, but Robert appeared unmoved.

"You have done your duty to a cripple, my dear," he said harshly. "There is no need to carry on about it."

"A cripple? Is that what you consider yourself? Well, you are right," Clare raged in a whisper. "You are a cripple, but not because of your injury. You are a cripple in your mind!" She whirled round and rushed across the room.

"Oh, dear, I must tend to Clare. I'm—I'm sorry, Robert," Sara said as she followed in her sister's wake.

A white-faced Robert stared straight ahead, blind to those around him. Edward and Richard exchanged looks before Richard grasped Robert's shoulder. "I believe my wife and I are ready to depart. Will you accompany us, Robert?"

After a moment of staring unblinkingly at his friend, Robert nodded. "Yes, I am ready to leave."

Edward awkwardly shook hands with Sir Robert. "I'm sorry for Clare's words. She was overset. She didn't mean what she said."

Though Robert took Edward's hand, he didn't acknowledge his friend's words. Diana and her two escorts crossed to the door, only to be intercepted by their hostess.

"What, you cannot be leaving already? Why, we have not yet had supper. I assure you I'm serving delightful lobster patties because I was told they were your favourite, Lord Rossley."

Richard stared at the woman, speechless. Diana again intervened. "Indeed, you are correct, Mrs. Sheffield, and it was most thoughtful of you to offer his favourite dish. However, my husband's doctor will not allow long evenings just yet. Lord Rossley wanted to come this evening, but he had to promise to make an early night of it."

"Oh, of course, we would do nothing to impede his recovery. You are our hero, my lord, and we all wish you well. You, also, Sir Robert. Are you departing as well?"

"Yes," Robert replied briefly.

"Sir Robert has contributed much to my husband's recovery. They are the best of friends." Diana smiled at the woman, hoping that would be the end of the questions. She couldn't guarantee polite behaviour from either of the men alongside her.

With only the briefest of goodbyes, they escaped their hostess and descended the outer steps to their coach, hastily summoned by the footmen.

"Will you let us drop you off at your lodgings?" Diana asked Robert.

"No, I have my own carriage here."

"Robert—" Diana began, but broke off as the man swung round to face her. The pain in his eyes clutched at her heart. "Robert, Clare was not pitying you this evening. She meant what she said about preferring to dance with you."

"Of course, Diana, any belle of the ball prefers to dance with a cripple who care barely manoeuvre around the fringes of the dance floor."

"Being belle of the ball becomes tiring. Dancing with someone you care about does not," Diana assured the infuriating man coldly. Turning, she entered the carriage and settled herself on the seat, refusing to look at the two men standing beside the carriage.

With a sigh, Richard said, "Let's meet at the club tomorrow about noon. We have a great deal to discuss."

Robert nodded and turned away.

Richard entered the carriage and sat down opposite his wife. "What an interesting evening," he finally remarked after the carriage had started up.

Diana shifted her gaze from the carriage window to the shadowy figure of the man opposite her. "Yes, wasn't it?"

A lengthy silence followed before Richard said, "Did you dance often while I was away?"

With a puzzled look, Diana replied, "I danced on occasion. Certainly not as often as Clare, who, as

Robert so delicately put it, is often the belle of the ball.''

"Did you often dance with Lord Anthony?"

"On occasion. He had always been friendly. After all, he is Aunt Margaret's godson."

"Ah. I had forgot that fact."

Diana drew her Valencia lace wrap about her as a shiver ran through her. She didn't understand the questions her husband was asking. But she recognized the tone of voice as one of danger.

"And did he escort you home?"

Diana stiffened, an explanation for his line of questioning finally occurring to her. "Do you mean, did he sleep in my bed?"

"Lady Rossley, where is your delicacy?" Richard snapped.

"It disappeared when I realized my husband was questioning my fidelity because I danced with another man this evening," she snapped in return.

"I meant no such—"

"If you have doubts about my behaviour, I suggest you question your servants, or perhaps your aunt, if you feel she can be trusted. Of course, such enquiries would not reflect well on you, but I'm sure that is of little consequence, my lord."

"Diana—"

"Do you not mean *madam?*"

"I refuse to argue with you," Richard said loftily, realizing there was no way he could win such an argument. "Because I choose to discuss the evening is no reason to attack me. Ladies of delicacy would never speak so, even to their husbands."

Diana leaned her head wearily against the velvet squabs of the coach. Why had she bothered? she wondered. Lord Rossley was correct: she had not behaved properly. Ladies did not fight for what they wanted. She should have accepted Robert's judgement of himself. She shouldn't have encouraged her husband's recovery. A lady would have left everything up to the gentlemen, no matter how wrong they might be.

When they reached their residence, Diana, first out of the carriage, of course, made for the stairs, determined not to linger for another bitter argument.

"Lady Rossley," Richard called out as she preceded him up the stairway. She stopped but did not turn round.

"I apologize for my words in the carriage."

Diana turned slowly on the fourth step. The footman who had opened the door stared straight ahead as if they were invisible. "It is of no matter, my lord." The weariness in her voice affected him.

He stepped up beside her and lowered his voice. "It was sad repayment for your support this evening, for which I am grateful."

Diana dropped her eyes. "It is a wife's duty."

He raised her hand to his lips and kissed it. "I hope you may never tire of your duty, my dear."

With a strangled good-night, Diana rushed up the stairs. Once she reached the sanctity of her room, she slumped against the door. *Duty!* As if her support of that infuriating man were only because it was her duty. When he had first returned, she had felt pity because of his injury—and curiosity. Each day spent with him had nourished a need for companionship, for caring, for that cherished dream of a real family.

She stepped away from the door and began to undress. She didn't want to admit that her cherished dream was changing. She wanted more: she wanted her husband to love her, to live with her as man and wife, to share the joys that life had given them. But he understood only her duty. Perhaps it was just as well. It kept her from being humiliated by his rejection.

RICHARD WATCHED HIS WIFE ascend the stairs. The woman was quite beautiful, he realized. Not in the sense that his first wife was beautiful; she had been the toast of the Season, her golden curls and blue eyes celebrated by every bachelor. Diana's beauty was different. She was attractive, but it was her grey eyes, their depth and integrity, that gave her face its unique beauty.

Those grey eyes had stayed with him, in the back of his mind, as he fought on the Continent. It was the only feature of his wife he could recall. And tonight, he had wounded her with his foolish questions. He had seen the pain and anger in her eyes.

Why he had bothered, he didn't know. He did not believe Diana would betray him as his first wife had done. And of course he wasn't jealous because she had danced with Lord Anthony. It must have been idle curiosity. Well, he had apologized, and he had more important thoughts to occupy his mind. Tomorrow morning he would meet with Robert and Edward and discuss their plans.

He ascended the stairs to prepare for bed. As he sank onto the feather mattress, his last thought was whether Lord Anthony had accompanied Lady Margaret and Diana often.

CHAPTER EIGHT

"I DON'T THINK last night could be considered a success," Edward said solemnly as the three gentlemen sat in the book room at Watier's.

Richard almost laughed at such an understatement. "I think that is fair to say."

"I told you I would be no good at such social functions." Robert's morose expression reflected his gloomy words.

"Well, I think part of the difficulty could be placed on our wives' shoulders," Edward suggested. "I have never known Sara to behave so poorly."

"I do not even *have* a wife," Robert said roughly.

"You have Clare to assist you," Richard offered, a slight grin on his face. "She seems determined to prod you as a wife would do."

"It is time you married that girl off to someone, Edward. I think you are remiss in your duty. This is almost the end of her second Season."

"Here, now. I'll have you know I've done my best. There have been many offers for her hand, but she keeps turning them all down. Why, some of them have been most advantageous." He shook his head. "I don't understand the girl. M'wife keeps saying Clare has the right to decide."

"She'll be an ape leader before long," Robert forecasted gloomily.

"Why don't you marry her?" Richard asked. A sudden longing to see Robert married had been born in him last evening when his wife showed so much concern for his friend.

"Do not be absurd. Clare deserves better than me."

"Oh, I think ape leaders must take what is offered, even someone such as you." Richard watched curiously as Robert glared at him.

"Clare is no ape leader! She is beautiful and…and wonderful. She may have her choice of men."

"You are the one who said she would soon be an ape leader," Richard said calmly.

"Richard has a point. She seems taken with you. Mayhap she'd accept an offer from you, Rob. And that'd get her off my hands." Edward looked around guiltily. "Not that I dislike having her about, but it is a worry trying to determine her future."

"You are both mutton-headed," Robert proclaimed harshly. "Clare will marry one day when the right man offers for her."

Silence fell. Suddenly Edward looked at the others with a grin on his face. "If you married her, Rob, you'd be a member of the family. I say, that's a wonderful idea. Why didn't I think of it before?"

"Because it is ridiculous!" Robert growled. "And it is nothing to do with why we are here this morning."

"I forgot," Edward said, shrugging his shoulders. "Oh, well, it was merely a suggestion. What do we do about our plan?"

"I think we must abandon any hope of progressing at evening entertainments. If we accompany our wives, we have duties to perform which will interfere."

"Right you are. Sara was not best pleased with me last evening," Edward said, looking uncomfortable.

"Besides, most of the gentlemen are taken up with pursuing the fairer sex at such events, or they wouldn't be there." A nod from both his companions confirmed Richard's opinion. "Therefore, we will do better work at our clubs or at small gatherings like our dinner party on Thursday. Perhaps we shall overhear talk of unusual increases in a merchant's business. And I believe my groom may be able to discover more by frequenting some of the taverns along the Thames. After all, if Napoleon is receiving English goods, they must be loaded on a ship somewhere."

"That's a good idea. I'll have my groom accompany yours." Robert looked vastly relieved. "And you'll not hear any complaints from me about not attending the balls."

"Nor from me. We never attend all the offerings of the Season. It tires Sara too much, and lately she appears exhausted much of the time. I'll recommend we cut back on our evenings out. That will leave me free to visit the clubs. After all, Sara won't expect me to sit home while she's tucked up in bed resting."

"Who will escort Clare?" Robert asked abruptly.

"I thought you weren't interested?" Richard asked, one eyebrow rising.

"I'm merely concerned for her. She is like . . . like a sister to me," Robert assured his friends, ignoring the flush in his cheeks.

NO COST! NO OBLIGATION TO BUY! NO PURCHASE NECESSARY!

PLAY "LUCKY 7" AND GET AS MANY AS SIX FREE GIFTS...

HOW TO PLAY:

1. With a coin, carefully scratch off the silver box at the right. This makes you eligible to receive one or more free books, and possibly other gifts, depending on what is revealed beneath the scratch-off area.

2. You'll receive brand-new Harlequin Regency Romance™ novels. When you return this card, we'll send you the books and gifts you qualify for *absolutely* free!

3. If we don't hear from you, every other month we'll send you 4 additional novels to read and enjoy. You can return them and owe nothing but if you decide to keep them, you'll pay only $2.64* per book, a savings of 31¢ each off the cover price. There is **no** extra charge for postage and handling. There are no hidden extras.

4. When you join the Harlequin Reader Service®, you'll get our monthly newsletter as well as additional free gifts from time to time just for being a subscriber.

5. You must be completely satisfied. You may cancel at any time simply by sending us a note or a shipping statement marked ''cancel'' or returning any shipment to us at our cost.

This lovely Victorian pewter-finish miniature is perfect for displaying a treasured photograph—and it's yours absolutely free—when you accept our no-risk offer.

PLAY "LUCKY 7"

Just scratch off the silver box with a coin. Then check below to see which gifts you get.

YES! I have scratched off the silver box. Please send me all the gifts for which I qualify. I understand I am under no obligation to purchase any books, as explained on the opposite page.

248 CIH ACKW

NAME

ADDRESS   APT

CITY   STATE   ZIP

7 7 7	WORTH FOUR FREE BOOKS, FREE VICTORIAN PICTURE FRAME AND MYSTERY BONUS
🍒🍒🍒	WORTH FOUR FREE BOOKS AND MYSTERY BONUS
●●●	WORTH FOUR FREE BOOKS
🔔🔔🍒	WORTH TWO FREE BOOKS

DETACH AND MAIL CARD TODAY

HARLEQUIN "NO RISK" GUARANTEE

- You're not required to buy a single book—ever!
- You must be completely satisfied or you may cancel at any time simply by sending us a note or a shipping statement marked "cancel" or returning any shipment to us at our cost. Either way, you will receive no more books; you'll have no obligation to buy.
- The free books and gifts you receive from this "Lucky 7" offer remain yours to keep no matter what you decide.

If offer card is missing write to: Harlequin Reader Service, 3010 Walden Ave., P.O. Box 1867, Buffalo, N.Y. 14269-1867

"Sara will find someone to chaperon her. Someone safe," Edward hurriedly added at Robert's stern look.

Richard brought them back to their reason for meeting. "Sir Toby will be at our dinner party. Have either of you talked to him yet?"

ANOTHER THREESOME was meeting at Edward's house. Clare was pouring tea as Sara relaxed on a chaise longue. Diana sat nearby, a frown on her face.

"I think you are doing too much, Sara," Diana suggested.

"Nonsense. I am fine. It is just that the early months are very tiring."

"All the more reason, sister, for you to curtail your social activities." Clare handed her a cup of tea with loving concern.

"But, Clare darling, you must have a chaperon. This is your second Season. If you don't find a husband this year, Mama may forbid your coming to us next year."

"I, for one, think you made some progress last evening," Diana said.

"I behaved badly. Mama would have been horrified," Clare said. "Much too forward for a well-behaved lady." She sniffed.

"Good behaviour is poor comfort to loneliness," Diana muttered.

"Yes," Sara agreed, fire in her eyes. "I made it clear to Edward that I did not appreciate being abandoned."

"I believe that is the way of husbands at such entertainments," Diana said.

"It is true that most husbands abandon their wives for the card room, but Edward does not leave me," Sara said proudly, before added, "until last evening. Do you suppose he no longer loves me?" Her plaintive question revealed her disquiet.

"You know that is not true," Diana reassured her. "It is just this silly secret which drew him from your side. I think the sooner we discover the reason, the better it would be. Richard is growing fatigued from so many outings."

"But we must wait until Thursday's dinner party to further our pursuit," Sara said with a sigh.

"Yes, but keep an eye on Edward's comings and goings and I shall do the same with Richard, and we may compare notes."

DIANA CAME DOWN EARLY to inspect the table arrangements one more time on the night of their first dinner party. She had never played hostess for her father, since he spent his evenings at one gambling den or another, and with her husband away, she had not entertained since her marriage. She wanted her first party to be perfect.

Her cream muslin gown with an apricot overdress had been carefully chosen to lend her an air of sophistication. The apricot colour also added a flush to her pale cheeks. With her hair elegantly coiffed by her maid, she hoped she would not disappoint her husband.

Boswell interrupted her contemplation of the table with its gleaming silver and crystal.

"My lady, Sir Robert has arrived."

"Already? My, he is early. Show him to the drawing-room and I'll join him there."

Diana made an adjustment to the centrepiece before turning to go to the drawing-room. Why had Robert come so early? Perhaps he hoped to meet with Richard. If they went to the study to talk, would she be bold enough to listen at the door? It was important to discover what they were about, but she wasn't sure she could bring herself to sink that low.

"Robert, welcome," Diana said as she entered the drawing-room.

He sprang from the chair he had taken and took her hand. "You are lovely this evening, Diana."

"Thank you, Robert. I'll take all the compliments I can get before Clare arrives. After that, I shall be invisible."

"Clare? I did not know she was coming," Robert said with a frown.

"Why, yes. I saw no reason not to include her. After all, Edward and Sara are coming."

"Yes, of course, it is just that I did not think she would enjoy such an evening when there were balls in the offing."

"I think you put too much emphasis on the frivolous aspects of Clare's nature. She is an intelligent young woman and enjoys a variety of events."

He turned away and walked over to the fire burning in the grate. "It has nothing to do with me. You are the hostess, after all."

Diana walked over to his side, forcing him to look at her. "It has everything to do with you, and well you know it. Why do you treat Clare as you do?"

"I don't know what you mean."

His frozen features did not fool Diana. In spite of the pain she saw in his eyes, she pressed on. "You have been pushing her away ever since you returned from the Continent. She cares for you, Robert."

"Don't!" Robert protested. When Diana stared at him, still waiting for an answer, he finally muttered, "It is a matter of honour."

"Honour?" Diana demanded, her hand on his arm. "Surely Clare's happiness is more important than honour?"

"No, it is not a question of her happiness—or rather it *is*. She is young and dreams of playing the martyr to a war hero. She will outgrow her infatuation, and when she does, it will be best if she is not tied to me."

Diana stared into Robert's eyes, sharing his pain, but also irritated at his hard-headedness. "Robert, you cannot deny your love. You must—"

"Am I intruding?" Richard's frosty words provoked differing responses in his audience. Robert was relieved that Diana could no longer probe into his painful feelings. Diana was irritated that her husband would interrupt just when she thought she might persuade Robert to act on those feelings.

Richard strolled into the room, outwardly calm, but inwardly raging. To find his wife in an intimate pose with another man, discussing his love, was a re-enactment of many scenes from his first marriage. The deeply burning anger at such betrayal from one he had begun to believe he might trust was all-encompassing.

"Is anything amiss? Your discussion seemed most serious," he prodded.

"No!" Robert exclaimed, alarmed that Diana might continue to pursue the matter in front of his friend.

"Of course not," Diana said at the same time. With a laugh at their simultaneous response, she continued, "We were discussing some of our guests."

"Oh? I thought I had read the guest list. I don't recall any extraordinary names on it."

Diana frowned. Her husband seemed intent upon making a point, but she did not understand exactly what it might have been. "I consider Sir Toby Bartholomew extraordinary." Perhaps this would be a good time to probe a little into the interesting list of guests her husband had given her. "To have come up through the ranks of the merchants and been knighted by Prinny is extraordinary. Is he a particular friend of yours, Richard?"

"An acquaintance only. Edward knows him better than I. He should add interest to the conversation this evening." Richard would not be put off the trail by such diversions. "Perhaps you and Robert were selecting topics to be discussed at dinner?"

Before Diana could respond to such a curious question, Robert rushed in. "Our conversation had nothing to do with dinner this evening."

In spite of Rob's flushed cheeks, Richard knew his friend would never betray him, particularly with his own wife. Diana, of course, was another matter. His first wife had taught him women were notoriously fickle. "Have you forgot the purpose of our party this evening, Robert?"

"Richard! What are you talking about?"

"Yes, Richard," Diana repeated, her interest rising appreciably, "just what *is* the purpose of the party this evening?"

It was Richard's turn to be confounded by their conversation. But he pulled himself together quickly. "Why, merely to enjoy ourselves, my dear. What else could it possibly be?"

His bland look did not fool his wife, but she realized the opportunity had passed. Lord Rossley would be difficult to trick. "I certainly hope so, my lord."

"Mr. and Mrs. White," Boswell announced. The trio turned in relief. Each for a different reason was pleased their small numbers were being expanded.

"Where is Clare?" Robert demanded before Diana even realized Sara's sister was not accompanying them.

"She'll be along later," Sara said. "Since we wanted to come early, the Rossiters offered to bring Clare with them."

"Damn it, Rob, if I don't think *you* should be Clare's guardian. You take more interest in her comings and goings than I do." Edward's chuckle was the only sound in the awkward pause which followed his words. Robert turned away, his face red.

Richard looked at his wife, watching her closely. If she were attracted to Rob, Edward's remarks should bring her pain. It would serve her right to be rejected by the one she had chosen in her betrayal.

"Sara, let me show you the centrepiece. I think perhaps it needs a little adjustment," Diana offered, hoping to distract everyone. She didn't mind that her suggestion offered an escape from masculine company for a few minutes.

Once the door was pulled to behind the two women, Diana told her friend, "We were right. The dinner party has some significance. Richard asked Robert if he had forgot the purpose of it."

"But what *is* the purpose?" Sara asked.

"I don't know. When I asked Richard that question, he refused to answer, assuring me it was for enjoyment only." She paused, thinking back over the conversation. "But he was acting very strangely. It was almost as if he were angry with Robert."

"Angry with Robert? What does that signify?" Sara asked, puzzled.

"I don't know." With a sigh, she added, "We only seem to discover more questions, rather than answers."

"Edward has said nothing, but he is constantly distracted." With a sniff, she added, "And he is spending less and less time with me and the children."

"Now, Sara, you mustn't cry," Diana said hurriedly. What would Edward say if she returned his wife to him with red eyes?

"Oh, it is just because I am increasing," Sara explained wearily. "It always makes me cry over n-nothing."

IN THE DRAWING-ROOM, Edward congratulated Richard on the future success of their evening, but Richard did not take his eyes from Robert.

"I'm not so sure our trio is a good idea," he said slowly.

"What?" Edward exclaimed. "What are you talking about?"

"I'm talking about my wife's interest in Rob."

Robert stared at his friend in stunned surprise. Edward, however, protested. "Richard, Robert would never betray you!"

"We are not speaking of Rob's behaviour, Edward, but of my wife's."

"If you are talking about our coze here when you arrived, that had nothing to do with Diana and myself. And if you doubt my word, you may name your seconds!" Robert challenged, his anger rising.

Edward quickly stepped between the two men. "Here now, none of that! What is he talking about, Robert? Surely this is all a mistake?" Edward's gaze swung back and forth between his two best friends.

"Of course it is a mistake. Diana was—was talking to me about Clare," Robert admitted reluctantly, looking away.

Richard flicked an imaginary piece of lint from his blue jacket. "I did not expect you to admit it. After all, an honourable man protects a lady's name even if she is at fault."

Enraged, Robert pushed against Edward, hoping to plant a facer on Richard's chin. "How dare you? How could you think that Diana would betray you in such a way? Diana has been faithful to your name without a word of gossip during your entire absence. If she had wanted to betray you, she wouldn't have had to wait until your return."

Such logic caught Richard's attention, but past aches made it difficult to accept.

"What makes you think Diana— What makes you suspicious?" Edward demanded.

"I entered the room to see them close together and Diana told him that he couldn't deny his love." Richard's clipped tones hid the pain he felt.

Edward turned to stare at Robert in consternation.

Responding to that look, Robert mumbled, "It is not what you think."

"I'm sure we are both willing to listen to your explanation," Edward suggested.

Robert ran his hand through his carefully arranged locks and paced about the room. "Diana was discussing my...my feelings for Clare." Edward started to speak and then stopped himself. "I was trying to tell her that it would be dishonourable to take advantage of Clare's infatuation."

"If you truly care—" Edward began eagerly.

Richard stared at his friend, unsure whether to believe his tale, but he didn't have an opportunity to express himself either way because of Boswell's next announcement.

"Sir Toby Bartholomew and Lady Bartholomew."

All three gentlemen snapped to attention. It was time to begin their duties, regardless of their personal feelings.

CHAPTER NINE

RICHARD DECIDED he was not cut out for the duty of ferreting out information which Lord Wyckham had assigned him. Discussion throughout dinner was impossible, seated as they were, ladies alternating with gentlemen. However, opportunity would come when the ladies withdrew, he reminded himself. It was just as well. He was much too distracted by his wife and friend, seated together at the other end of the table.

He maintained an effortless conversation with Lady Bartholomew, consisting of innocuous comments of "Really?" or "How interesting," inserted when that lady paused to draw breath. With the rest of his energies, he watched Diana charm Sir Toby, seated to her right. He also took note of the fact that she seldom spoke at all to Robert, leaving him to the tender care of Clare, seated beside him.

Could Robert have been telling the truth? Had his wife been faithful? Time would tell. He intended to keep a close watch on her. This time, if his wife chose to hold him up to the ton for ridicule, he would divorce her, no matter how much scandal it caused.

Lost in his thoughts, it was not until Lady Bartholomew nudged him and whispered, "Her ladyship is looking this way," that he realized his wife was waiting for his signal for the women to withdraw.

After the women left the room, Richard invited the men to gather down at his end of the table and motioned for Boswell to begin serving the brandy.

As an opening gambit, Richard asked, "Has anyone heard the latest news of the war today?"

In no time at all, the gentlemen were involved in a discussion of the war and its effect on England, providing their host ample opportunity to defend his country's manner of conducting war.

TEA AND GOSSIP were the order of the evening in the drawing-room as the ladies awaited the men's appearance. Lady Bartholomew and several others on the fringe of Society were most interested in discovering the particular shops that their hostess frequented and in discussing the latest fashion. The subject turned to more domestic matters once those topics had been exhausted. Clare, with little interest in linens and children, kept her eyes fixed on the drawing-room door, watching for Robert's return.

When the wait seemed overlong, she turned to her hostess, silently asking her question with the lifting of one eyebrow and a look to the door. Diana, also, had been wondering what was keeping the gentlemen. She excused herself and slipped out into the hallway.

"Boswell?" she called in a low voice at the door to the butler's pantry, but he did not respond.

Just as she was considering searching further, Boswell opened the door to the dining-room. As soon as he had shut it behind him, Diana whispered, "Boswell, what is taking so long?"

"My lady, is anything amiss?"

"Nothing other than that we appear to have been abandoned by the gentlemen."

"Lord Rossley did not warn you?" Boswell asked, surprised.

"Warn me about what?"

"He told me they would be some time in the dining-room and that I must be sure to have plenty of spirits on hand."

Diana frowned as she considered his words. So their lingering at the table had been planned, but to what purpose? "Has Lord Rossley, Mr. White or Sir Robert left the table?"

"No, my lady." He paused before adding with a grin, "They are in the centre of the discussion because the topic is the war on the Continent."

"Ah. Very well, I shall encourage the ladies to be patient."

"Would you like me to serve the teacakes now? I do not believe the gentlemen will care for any after all the brandy."

"An excellent idea, Boswell. Can you manage to do so without disrupting service in the dining-room?" Diana asked.

"Of course, my lady. I'll have several footmen assist me."

Diana slipped back into the drawing-room. She gave a minute shake of her head to Clare and settled herself back on the sofa next to Lady Bartholomew.

"The men are talking war, I suppose, my dear?" Lady Bartholomew asked.

"Why, yes, I believe they are," Diana replied, surprised by her guest's perspicacity. "I hope you do not mind the delay in their joining us."

"Oh, I'm accustomed to it. My Toby discusses the war wherever we go, and the ladies are usually left to entertain themselves."

Diana gave the woman a warm smile, finding her likeable. "I shall ask Clare to play for us, then, and Boswell is going to serve some delicious teacakes. Perhaps that will serve as entertainment."

"I believe it will, my dear," the lady replied with a chuckle. "Thank goodness my Toby likes a lady well-rounded, because I fear I have no resistance to teacakes."

Diana put her plan into action, with Clare's and Boswell's assistance. When the gentlemen finally appeared over an hour later, they discovered the ladies enjoying themselves with no hint of impatience.

Richard, pleased with the conversation just finished, shared a look of triumph with Robert and Edward until he remembered the suspicions he harboured concerning his wife. He was somewhat mollified when Robert went immediately to Clare's side, volunteering to turn the pages of her music. But he still was not entirely satisfied.

DIANA WEARILY TRACED the rim of her teacup with one finger as she considered her day. There were the remains of the cleaning necessary from last evening's entertainment to be supervised. She needed to visit her dressmaker for the last fitting on a ball gown she had purchased the week before, and she thought it best to call on Sara this morning.

She should never have told Sara of her suspicions, but she hadn't realized how upsetting it would be for her. If, as she suspected, her husband and his friends were only supporting their King and country through talk about the war, praising the current administration's handling of it, then she had worried Sara needlessly. And Diana was almost sure that was their objective. The margin of doubt was small, but still it bothered her. But she should not allow Sara a peep at her doubts. She would—

"Mama!" a joyful little voice called as Melly scampered through the door to the breakfast room. Behind her came Nanny at a slower pace.

"I am sorry, my lady," Nanny huffed, coming to a halt in the doorway. "She insisted on asking if she could join you."

Diana received the soft, wriggling body in her arms and smiled at Nanny. "Melly's company is just what I needed, Nanny. I shall bring her up after we have breakfast together."

After Nanny had left the room, Melly's blond curls were shaken back and a pouty face stared up at Diana.

"You didn't come to see me last evening."

"No, darling, I didn't because we had our first party. I had too much to do."

"Papa didn't come see me either. Where is he?"

Diana busied herself seating Melly beside her and ringing for Boswell. "I don't know, darling. Perhaps Papa is still asleep." When the butler answered her summons, Diana said, "Boswell, does Cook have something special Lady Melanie would enjoy for breakfast? And bring her a pot of chocolate."

With a treat in store, Melanie was easily led to safer topics, those of her toys and her fifth birthday party. In only a month, she would be five years old and Diana had promised her a splendid celebration.

In the midst of their discussion, Lord Rossley entered the breakfast room, drawing up short when he observed its occupants.

"What? Have I made a mistake and gone to the nursery instead of the breakfast room?" he asked in mock astonishment.

"Papa," Melly protested with a giggle, "you know you have not. You are teasing me."

Coming around the table, he bent to kiss the forehead of his child before seating himself across from her. "Surely not, Lady Melanie. A gentleman never teases a lady."

"Oh, Papa!" she protested with more giggles.

When his gaze switched to the silent young woman seated beside Melly, his expression grew more reticent. "Good morning, my lady."

She nodded but kept her eyes on her second cup of tea.

"Papa?" Melly asked but waited until his gaze returned to her. "Why do you call Mama 'my lady'? Don't you know her name?"

"Of course I do, but it is perfectly proper to call her my lady. That is her title, you know," Richard responded, his cheeks flushed.

"Nicholas's papa calls his mama by her name," Melly said thoughtfully, before suddenly breaking into giggles. "Unless he calls her *my precious,*" she said, imitating Edward's voice.

"Melanie, a lady does not parody others," Richard said sternly.

The sunshine fled from the child's face as she returned to her earlier pout. "But he *does,* Papa. I heard him!"

"Your father means you should not pretend to *be* Mr. White when you repeat his words," Diana explained quietly.

"Oh, I'm sorry, Papa."

Boswell entered with a fresh pot of tea and Richard gratefully took the cup offered to him.

"May I serve you some eggs, my lord? Kippers?"

"Yes, Boswell, everything. I'm prodigiously hungry this morning."

Diana kept her eyes lowered, but she was happy over her husband's appetite. When he had first begun eating breakfast downstairs, he had had to be tempted to taste anything.

After Boswell withdrew, Melly, with the persistence of a child, asked, "What *do* you call Mama?"

There was a pause as two adult minds hastened to unscramble a child's logic. Lord Rossley took a stab. "I called her 'my lady.'"

"No, not now. I mean what do you call Mama when you want to love her?"

Diana choked on her tea and mopped up the hot liquid she'd spilt without looking at anyone.

A cold voice interrupted her activity. "Madam, you assured me you were supervising the care of my daughter. Is this how you think young ladies should behave?"

With a sigh, Diana looked at his rigid features. "No, my lord, I do not think Melly's question proper for polite conversation. But I have always encouraged her to speak freely to me. How else is a child to learn if she cannot ask questions?" She paused, but when Richard seemed unable to speak, she added, "But I have always emphasized that those conversations must be only between Melly and myself."

"And Papa, too," Melly insisted. "You said only in our *family*, Mama, and Papa is part of our family."

Still Richard remained silent, his face a frozen mask.

"Yes, darling, of course he is, but gentlemen...sometimes gentlemen don't enjoy talking quite as much as ladies. So perhaps it would be better if we only talked to each other about certain subjects."

"No!" Richard burst out. "I do not wish to be unapproachable," he continued, moderating his voice, "but I do not think Melly should question me about my personal activities."

"What your papa is saying, I believe, is that he loves you, Melly, and does not want you to be afraid to ask him a question if you need to know something, but that it is impolite to ask your father about his own behaviour." Diana kept her voice on an even keel, successfully hiding the hysteria rising just below the surface.

"Yes, that is exactly what I meant. Thank you...Diana."

Lady Melanie toyed with her pastry, her face gloomy. "I'm sorry, Papa. I thought since Nicholas's papa called his mama that in front of everyone, it would not be improper to ask."

Diana smiled in relief as she finally realized what Melanie had been asking. "My lord, I believe Melly simply wants to know if you have a...a pet name for me as Edward does for Sara."

"That *is* what I asked," Melly complained.

Diana's gaze met Richard's and she hurried to hide her smile. With a wry look in her direction, Richard said, "I didn't realize that, sweetheart. I'm sorry."

"So, may I ask that question?"

"As long as we are just among family, of course you may. Only...only, I have been back such a short time, I have not, er, actually..."

"He calls me 'my dear,' Melly."

"Do you like that?" Melly looked sceptical.

"Of course I do. If you are someone's dear, that means the same as being someone's precious," Diana explained with a smile.

"Oh, all right."

"I'm going to ring for Boswell and have a footman take you upstairs to Nanny. I have some errands to run and I think you may accompany me, if you like."

"Oh, yes, Mama. May I wear my pink dress?"

"You may, sweet child. I'll be ready in a little while."

Melly jumped down from her chair as Boswell entered. After Diana gave her orders, Melly hugged her neck. "Thank you, my dear," she said in grown-up tones before breaking into giggles. She repeated the hug with her father, "Goodbye, my dear," before scampering from the room.

"I am grateful you gave her a simple appellation in response to her question, or we might have been highly embarrassed in public."

"Melly's public behaviour is always above reproach," Diana assured him stiffly.

"I did not intend to criticize. Rather, I was offering praise for your handling of a difficult situation," Richard assured her with a sigh.

"Thank you," she muttered as she stood.

"Where are you going?"

"As I told Melly, I have errands to run this morning. I thought I would prepare to go out."

"Might I have your attention for a few moments first?" he asked, the formality in his voice putting Diana on guard.

"If you wish. Shall I await you in the study?"

"It is nothing so formal, my dear," he said without thinking. When their gazes met and the two of them burst into laughter, the formality dissolved.

Diana sat down again and waited with a more relaxed air for her husband to speak.

"I wished to congratulate you on a marvellous party last evening."

"Thank you."

Richard ran a finger around the folds of his cravat, as if it were too tight, before he said, "I wondered if we might have another such party soon?"

"I have no objection," Diana replied. "However, I feel I must include certain people in our next party."

"Of whom are you speaking?" Richard asked, a frown on his face.

"It is simply that last night was our first entertainment and we did not include the only members of your family in London. While I might explain away such an insult this time, I could not do so a second time."

"I only know of one relation of mine in London," Lord Rossley said icily.

"You have two, my lord," Diana said calmly, waiting for the storm to break.

He did not disappoint her. "How dare you call that woman a member of my family! She shall *not* be invited to any party of which I am the host. Do you hear me?"

"Shall we adjourn to the study?" Her quiet voice only emphasized his sizzling, strident tones.

"Do not think you can persuade me to invite that woman here, because you cannot! Just because you forced me to agree to occasional outings with her for Melly does not mean—"

"Very well, my lord," Diana said, surprising her adversary as she walked from the room.

"Madam! Come back here! I will not—" He stopped when it was clear she had no intention of obeying him.

"AUNT MARGARET, I have come to you for assistance," Diana said quietly as Melly played with a wooden toy Lady Margaret's butler had carved for her.

"Ah. Shall I ask Elkins to show Melly some other projects he has?"

"If you do not mind." Diana had added one more chore to her list after breakfast with Lord Rossley: a visit to his aunt, Lady Margaret Hanson.

Once the child had left the drawing-room, Diana began her tale of woe. "You have heard we had a dinner party last evening?"

"Yes, I did hear of it." There was a light stiffness in the woman's voice.

"It was of such short notice and the guests such a mixture that I did not invite you for fear you'd be bored to death."

"I am seldom bored."

Diana rose to her feet and paced. "The truth is, Aunt Margaret, that I was so concerned with Richard that I did not think. I apologize."

The elderly woman leaned forward intently. "What do you mean, 'concerned with Richard'?"

"Oh, I believe it is nothing now, but—but I overheard him and his friends talk about once again serving their King and country, and I panicked. I thought he was doing something to endanger himself."

"But he is not?" the old lady asked anxiously.

"No, I'm sure he is not. I believe he is merely supporting the government's handling of the war by talking to those in Society and encouraging them to lend their support."

"Ah. Was that the purpose of the party?"

"I believe so. Anyway, I was so distracted that I did not think about it being our first entertainment and how it would look if we ignored the only relations either of us have in London."

"I notice you use the plural."

Diana sat back down on the sofa and grimaced. "Yes, of course. Richard also noticed. That is when the fireworks began."

"What is the difference now? We shall find a reason for our not being included and the next time you entertain, you may rectify the matter."

"But that is the problem, Aunt Margaret. Richard wishes to entertain again, soon, I believe for the same purpose. But when I suggested we invite you and Hetta, he became enraged."

"You mean he objected to *my* presence?" Lady Hanson teased.

Diana gave a half-hearted grin. "Of course not." Finally she had come to the reason for her visit. "What shall I do?"

"Hmm." Lady Hanson leaned back in her chair, narrowing her eyes in thought. "Not an easy question, my dear."

"No."

"Well, I will talk to the boy, of course. But I cannot guarantee he will listen."

"Thank you, Aunt Margaret. I don't know what I'd do without you."

"You'd muddle through, child. And how are you and Richard getting along, aside from Hetta, of course?"

Diana ducked her head and adjusted the lace on her cuff. "Just fine, thank you. Richard's health is much improved. Just this morning he breakfasted—"

"I don't want to know what the boy eats. I want to know if he has recognized you as his wife."

"Why, of course he has," Diana assured her. "I was hostess at our party."

"Not in public! Don't try to fob me off with foolish answers. What is happening in the bedchamber?"

Diana's cheeks turned red. "Aunt Margaret—"

"You want to tell me it's none of my business." The elderly woman sat ramrod straight, but her chin quivered as she admitted, "I love that boy more than anyone in the world, even more than you and Melly. He's the son I never had. I want him to be happy."

Diana reached out and clasped one of Lady Hanson's hands. "Aunt Margaret, I love him also. I didn't intend to do so, but he is . . . is lovable in spite of his temper. But such things take time. You cannot expect us to . . . that is, we do not . . ."

Lady Hanson rescued her from her floundering. "All right, child. I understand. But it is unnatural for a man and wife—oh, very well, but I'll have you know I would like more family members before much longer."

DIANA WAS RELIEVED when their carriage pulled away from Lady Margaret's house. It had been a most difficult interview. And now she faced another: Sara would not be easily appeased.

"Mama? Are we going to see Nicholas and Sara now?"

Melly's question wakened Diana from her musing. "Yes, love, we're going to the Whites' now."

"I think I should not tell Papa anything Nicholas says any more," the child said with little-girl wisdom.

"What do you mean, Melly?"

"He didn't like it when I talked about another baby, and he became upset when I asked what he called you."

"Um, yes, well, Papa just didn't understand what you meant this morning."

Melly thought about Diana's explanation before saying, "I know, but I think I'll just talk to *you* about what Nicholas says."

"That might be best, sweetheart. Sometimes men just don't understand."

CHAPTER TEN

"Do you truly believe they are in no danger?" Sara asked, her pale cheeks worrisome to her friend.

"Truly, Sara. And I am sorry I disturbed you with my silly suspicions," Diana added. She hoped telling Sara the men were simply supporting the government in the conversations would relieve some of the strain so visible in Sara's eyes.

"That is good news, isn't it, Sara?" Clare said encouragingly. "Now you know that whatever Edward is doing, he is not in danger."

"Yes, that is good news," Sara said, but there was no spark of happiness in her wan face.

Diana and Clare exchanged concerned looks. "Have you told Edward yet that there will be an addition to your family?" Diana asked.

"No."

"I believe you should tell him at once," Clare said. "He is so careful of Sara's comfort when she is increasing. It is very touching."

"He would not be this time. He is too occupied with whatever he is doing," Sara said despondently.

"Sara, have you had your doctor visit you?" Diana asked.

"No. My doctor, the one I used with Nicholas and Sally, died last year. I haven't chosen a doctor for this baby."

"May I recommend Doctor Brownell, who tended Richard? He told me he attends lying-ins."

"Oh, Diana, it is months before I must have a doctor poking about. I shall decide later," Sara said as she lay back against the pillows.

"But I think you should see a doctor now, Sara. You don't appear in your normal state of health."

Such tender concern released Sara's frail control. "I am not," she wailed. "I am increasing!"

Clare gathered the weeping form into her arms and comforted her. After whispered consultation with her friend, Diana summoned the butler. She soon sent him on his way with a brief message for Doctor Brownell. Then she assisted Clare in urging Sara to her bed. Within half an hour, Doctor Brownell had responded to her message and visited Mrs. White in her bed-chamber with her friend and sister in attendance.

Afterwards, he accepted the offer of a cup of tea in the drawing-room with Clare and Diana.

"I believe you were right to call me, Lady Ross-ley," Doctor Brownell said as he sipped his tea. "Mrs. White appears to be under a great deal of strain, and in her condition, I advise complete bedrest for a week. After such time, she may return to limited activities, but the full schedule for the Season is not to be contemplated." He turned to Clare. "Do you reside here with your sister?"

"Yes, I do, and you may rest assured I will see to it that she follows your orders."

"And her husband?"

Clare exchanged an uneasy glance with Diana. "You see, Doctor, her husband does not know about...about the baby, and I am reluctant to tell him without Sara's agreement."

"Humph! Seems to me an observant husband would have noticed his wife was out of frame."

"Truly, he usually is most attentive to Sara, but he is involved with Lord Rossley and Sir Robert in some activity that has drawn his attention from his family."

The door to the drawing-room swung open and three men walked in, their outdoor vigour and shared laughter at odds with the quiet concern in the drawing-room.

"Oh, hello, Diana, Clare. Where's Sara?" Edward asked carelessly.

The other two men were more formal in their greetings and each avoided a certain female's eyes.

Clare, acting as hostess, said, "Edward, may I present Doctor Brownell? Doctor, this is my sister's husband. And with him are Sir Robert and Lord Rossley."

"Good day, gentlemen," the doctor said, rising. "I, of course, am acquainted with Lord Rossley."

Edward frowned as he bowed to the doctor. "Why are you here? One of the children not feeling well?"

"No, sir, I have not attended your children."

"Sara called you for one of the servants?"

The doctor studied the man with interest. "No, sir, I have not attended your servants."

The panic in Edward's eyes was reassuring to several people in the drawing room. "Sara? You are here for Sara? Where is she?" he demanded even as he spun round to run from the room.

"Might I speak with you in private, sir?" Doctor Brownell asked.

Lord Rossley grabbed his friend by the arm and halted his retreat. "Doctor, is Sara all right?"

"At the moment, my lord, I believe she is resting comfortably."

"Edward, go with the doctor. He has said Sara is quite well," Richard assured his friend.

Edward's panic subsided and he reluctantly led the doctor from the room. Clare quietly offered cups of tea to the newcomers.

"What about Sara?" Robert demanded even as he took his cup.

Again Clare and Diana exchanged glances. "She is fine," Clare said calmly.

"Then why the doctor?" Richard demanded harshly. Sara was a favourite of his and he did not intend to be put off by platitudes.

"Richard, Sara is in no danger, and it is up to Edward or Sara to discuss the . . . the difficulty with their friends," Diana said to assist Clare.

"But you know?"

"Yes, I know," Diana replied, her chin raised as she stared down her husband.

"Have you been to your club this morning?" Clare asked, desperately searching for a neutral subject.

"Yes," Robert answered shortly.

"What entertainment do you have planned for this evening?"

"Probably a return to Watier's," Robert said absently, his mind on the puzzle of Sara.

"You are not attending the Larrabys' musicale?"

"God forbid. I detest what is called music these days," Robert said.

"Clare, will you accompany me this evening? I don't think Sara will be able to chaperon you," Diana offered.

"Oh, thank you, Diana, that will be lovely if I am not needed here. I hadn't thought of that."

"The two of you cannot go alone," Richard protested.

"I don't see why not, but if you feel we should not, I'll write a note to Lord Anthony and ask if he will escort us."

Both men glared at Diana. Finally, Richard, sarcasm lacing his words, said, "Why would you think of Lord Anthony before your husband, my dear?"

"Because, *my dear,*" Diana replied tightly, "You have been in Robert and Edward's company every waking moment since you left your sickbed. If Robert is returning to Watier's for the evening, I assumed you also would return to Watier's."

While husband and wife glared at each other, Robert drew everyone's attention. "I shall escort the two ladies to the Larrabys'."

Clare, instead of being ecstatic as she would have been only a few days earlier, demanded coldly, "Why do you change your mind? You just said you detested musicales."

"I changed my mind because Edward is my friend. He will not want to leave Sara and yet you are his responsibility."

"There is no need," Clare replied, the word "responsibility" rankling. "Diana has just said she would enlist the services of Lord Anthony."

Richard wondered if Robert's sudden capitulation was also motivated by the jealousy that invaded him at the mention of Lord Anthony. "Never fear, Robert. I shall accompany my wife this evening."

Diana's eyebrows rose, but she accepted his proclamation calmly. "Why don't you join us, Robert? Then we shall have even numbers."

Richard frowned at his wife, causing her to wonder what she could possibly have done wrong. She assumed he would enjoy his friend's company.

"Thank you, Diana. At least *someone* appreciates my invitation," Robert said, cutting his eyes to Clare.

"*Some* thought it sounded more like a sacrifice than an invitation, and I have no taste for martyrs," Clare snapped.

Since Clare's normal tone when she addressed Robert was one of delight, endearment and joy, all were stunned, particularly Robert.

"Then perhaps it would be best if I do not accompany you," he replied sharply.

"I should remain at home. Sara might have need of me," Clare suggested in turn, a frown returning to her brow.

"You know that would only disturb Sara. She is in no danger. And we would enjoy your company, Robert." Diana's firm tones settled the matter. Before more difficulties arose, Diana stood. "Now that our evening is settled, I believe I'll collect Melly and go home. Give Sara my love, Clare."

"If you do not mind, I shall accompany you," Richard said, rising with her. "I rode with Robert. It will save him a drive."

"Of course." She paused, looking at the other two. "Robert, are you leaving now?"

"I thought I would wait and talk to Edward." His curious look turned to comprehension when Diana stared first at him and then at Clare.

"Of course, I had not thought," he hurriedly added. "I'll leave also."

Clare stared at the three of them. "Surely you are not suggesting I may not entertain Robert? I have known him forever. He is Edward's best friend."

"Clare, if someone in the ton found you alone with Robert, it would endanger your reputation," Diana said quietly. "As Sara's friend, I should feel responsible."

"Have no fear," Clare said grimly. "I shall retire to my chamber and leave Robert to wait in peace." Without another word, she swept from the room.

IN THE CARRIAGE, Melly, delighted to be joined by her papa, chattered away about the beautiful day and the fine horses she saw, but Diana noted with amusement that she did not once mention Sally and Nicholas.

Richard listened to his daughter for a few minutes and then turned to Diana. "Will you tell me what is amiss with Sara?"

Surprised, Diana stared at her husband. "I cannot, Richard. That is for Edward to say, or Sara."

"Surely they would not advocate your keeping something from your husband."

Diana stared straight ahead, refusing to answer such a ridiculous question. It was not as if she and Richard ever exchanged intimate thoughts or knowledge. If he preferred to treat her like a stranger, then he must not expect any different treatment for himself.

When they arrived home, Boswell met them as they entered the hall.

"Lady Hanson has called, my lord, and is awaiting your return in the parlour."

"Please tell her we shall join her at once."

Diana ignored his plural response and continued up the stairs with Melly.

"My lady."

Diana turned at her husband's call and looked down the stairs.

"Yes, my lord?"

"Have you no desire to speak with my aunt?"

"I have already visited Aunt Margaret today. I believe she called to see you."

Something in her words must have alerted Lord Rossley, for his eyes narrowed and he said in a dangerously smooth voice, "I believe I must request your presence in the parlour, my dear."

Melly, watching this by-play with concern, suddenly smiled. "You are right, Mama. He *does* call you 'my dear.' "

"Yes, darling, I know. Boswell, will you send a footman to accompany Lady Melanie to Nanny?" She knelt and hugged her stepdaughter. "Thank you for accompanying me today, my sweet. I enjoyed your company."

"I love you, Mama," the little girl said, hugging her neck. Then she peered down the stairs at the stern man watching them. "'Bye, Papa. I love you, too."

As the two females in his family continued up the stairs, Richard stared after them, unexpectedly touched by the open-hearted affection his daughter offered. For some inexplicable reason, it called to mind the moment when his wife had suggested inviting Lord Anthony to accompany her this evening. The jealousy— His mind came to an abrupt halt. He shook his head as if to clear it. Of course, it was not jealousy of his wife's affections. It couldn't be that. It was simply jealousy of his position in Society.

"My lord?" Boswell asked, wondering if there was something for which his lordship was waiting.

"What? Oh, nothing, Boswell. Here, take my hat and cane and I will go into the parlour. Show my wife into the parlour as soon as she appears and bring a tea tray."

"Very good, my lord."

WHEN A RELUCTANT DIANA entered the parlour, her husband and Lady Margaret were calmly chatting about the latest on-dits of the Season.

Her entry was followed immediately by a generous tea tray, including the macaroons that were Lady Hanson's favourites. After enjoying them for several contented minutes, Lady Margaret said, "I commend you on your re-entry into Society, my boy."

"Thank you, Aunt Margaret."

"I was afraid you'd be a recluse when you emerged from the sickroom. Your dinner party was a wonderful surprise."

Richard simply nodded and sipped his tea.

"Of course, I received many questions as to why I was not invited," the old lady said briskly.

Richard looked up, surprised. "It never occurred to me—that is, it was a gathering of men involved in the war effort."

"I understand. Diana was kind enough to explain that to me."

Giving his wife a quick look, Richard smiled charmingly at his aunt. "I assure you you will be invited to our next entertainment."

"And when shall that be? Want to mark it on my calendar."

"Why, I thought we might have another small dinner party next week," Richard said, keeping his smile in place with an effort. He sensed impending trouble.

With an air of deep thought, Lady Margaret said, "Wednesday would be convenient for me. Perhaps Wednesday?"

Richard and Diana both nodded, but Richard noticed his wife kept her eyes lowered.

"Good. I'll confer with Hetta. I'm sure she'll be free, also."

Richard stared at his aunt and then his wife. With ice in his voice, he said, "I do not believe I mentioned Mrs. Chadwell's name."

"What's the matter with you, boy? Are you losing your mind?"

Wondering if perhaps his aunt was correct, Richard glared at her. "No, I am not. I might believe I were if I invited that woman to my house."

Instead of appearing offended or angered, Lady Margaret shook her head sadly at her only kin. "Dear boy, I know you have scarce recovered from your wound, but—"

"I have completely recovered!" Richard shouted as he held his left arm close to his body to hide its limited movement.

"Richard," Diana murmured softly, her hand touching his right arm. "Aunt Margaret didn't mean to offend you, *my dear*," she said, hoping those words would diffuse his anger.

Shaken by his loss of temper, Richard stared down at the delicate hand resting on his blue superfine jacket. He raised his gaze to stare into Diana's calm grey eyes. A small smile tugged at his lips and he said, "Yes, my dear."

Diana returned his smile, the warmth in her expression lighting up her face, and Richard felt drawn to her, his eyes resting on her curved lips.

"She's right, boy. You've done marvellously well. But if you don't invite Hetta Chadwell, you're going to stir up all that old gossip."

Richard turned his gaze to his aunt. "Society must say what it will. I'll not invite that woman to my table."

"Richard, who do you think will suffer the most if gossip about your first wife remains alive?" Diana asked quietly.

"Mrs. Chadwell, I would suppose, since it was her daughter's behaviour which brought about the catastrophe." His coldness didn't augur well for their plan, but Diana persisted.

"You are wrong, my dear. It won't be Hetta who will suffer, or even yourself, very much. If that gossip is not allowed to die a natural death but is kept alive by your hatred and avoidance of Hetta, it is Melly who will suffer."

"Melly? No, I'll not allow it!" Richard roared.

"Then you must invite Hetta to your party and pretend a mending of your fences." Lady Margaret nodded at her nephew and selected another macaroon as if the matter were settled.

Richard turned away from Diana's sympathetic look and rose to stride over to the window and stare out at the busy London traffic. "I vowed never to speak to that woman again," he ground out in a low voice.

"Richard," Diana said, rising to join him, "I understand the pain you suffered because of your first marriage." When he would have objected, she added in a low voice, "Don't forget to whom you speak. Pain is our most common bond."

A grimace met her rueful smile. "Would you invite your father to tea, my dear?" he asked harshly.

Diana tried to ignore the tears that filled her eyes as she bit her lip to gain control. "Yes, my lord, I would. He did not intend to cause me pain, just as Hetta did not. And both suffered. I don't have the opportunity to extend my hand to my father," she said, gulping back the emotions that threatened to overcome her, "but I should do so if I could."

He stared down at her, silent. He looked over at his aunt, her back to them, contentedly munching macaroons, and then wrapped his right arm round his wife's shoulders.

Surprised, Diana sheltered against his lean frame, peace settling over her.

With his head resting on her silken hair and his nostrils flaring as he inhaled the lavender scent of her, Richard whispered, "I would not invite my wife, were she alive today, but perhaps I can manage the presence of her mother at my table if you place her far away from me."

In a bold gesture, Diana encircled her husband with her arms and kissed his cheek. "Thank you, Richard. It is most generous of you."

He stared down at her. Damning his left arm, he withdrew his right one from her shoulders to lift her chin and kissed the warm mouth that had been tempting him for the past few days.

The delicious excitement that careened through Diana shortened her breath and she backed away from him in astonishment, her grey eyes large, her lashes blinking rapidly. "I—I believe I shall look in on Melly," she whispered before fleeing from the room.

RICHARD PACED THE PARLOUR, waiting for his wife's appearance. After their visit with Lady Hanson, she had remained in her chamber for the rest of the day. Now they were on their way to the Whites' to collect Clare for the Larrabys' musicale.

Hearing a step, Richard raced to the door and looked up the stairs. Diana, more beautiful than he had ever seen her, was descending, the skirt of her peach evening gown sweeping the steps as she did so.

The kiss he'd given her earlier that day had been intended as comfort and gratitude. But before Diana had backed away from him, it had erupted into desire. Surprised by its intensity, Richard had waited for Diana's appearance to prove to himself that he had no feelings for the woman. Feelings led to pain, and he would not be caught in that trap again.

Now he stared at the vision before him and almost groaned aloud at the quickening of his heartbeat. *No,* he sternly admonished himself. *It is not too late. Just keep your distance from her.*

Diana watched the changes on Richard's face as she came down the stairs. She had been confused by his kiss earlier, but having regained her composure, she felt a delicious shiver of anticipation for the evening ahead of her. As she reached Richard's side, she extended her hand. When he ignored her gesture and turned his back on her, she almost crumpled in disappointment.

"Richard? Is anything wrong?"

"No, of course not." His harsh words echoed in the large foyer. "We are late and must hurry."

He stood back to allow Diana to precede him. After a moment's hesitation, she did so. But she left behind her hopes for a wonderful evening.

When they reached the Whites' house, Richard descended and left it to the footman to extend a helping hand to Diana. She gave her husband a puzzled look that he ignored as they marched up the steps to the door.

When they were shown into the parlour, Richard was relieved to find Edward waiting for them. "I appreciate your chaperoning Clare this evening," he said warmly.

"Sara is all right?" Richard asked.

"Diana didn't tell you? I was sure she would."

Avoiding her husband's eyes, Diana hurriedly said, "I thought you would enjoy the telling, Edward."

"True," he agreed, beaming at his friend. "Sara is increasing. In six months' time, I shall be a father again."

Richard congratulated Edward, shaking his hand.

"Of course, I shall have to cut back on my own activities," Edward said with an apologetic look at Richard. "I must support Sara at such a time, you understand."

"Of course," Richard agreed, though he was not sure he did.

"We will be able to attend a few functions, but Sara must rest."

"Sir Robert," the butler intoned. Robert entered immediately afterwards and again congratulated his friend, but Diana noted he seemed in no better humour than Richard.

"Where is Clare?"

"She has not yet descended, Robert. Don't tell me you are anxious to arrive on time at the musicale. Have you become an enthusiast for Italian sopranos now?" Edward teased, his happy smile indicative of his good humour now that the cause of Sara's illness was revealed.

Robert blanched. "Surely the same woman is not singing tonight?"

"Of course. She is all the rage."

Diana thought for a moment Robert was going to turn tail and desert them, but he straightened his shoulders and glared at Richard. "At least you will not be able to creep out early as you did last time, Richard. I shall have company in my misery."

"What a charming thought for our evening," Clare said from the doorway.

"I never pretended to like Italian opera singers," Robert protested.

"Or my company, it appears," the young woman replied coldly, though Diana could see nothing to dislike about Clare's appearance. In her silver gown and sapphire necklace, she looked like a fairy.

"Don't be a noddy, Clare. I said nothing about your company."

"I am not accustomed to being called a noddy, Sir Robert," Clare returned, her nose in the air.

With her own hopes and dreams already shattered, Diana watched what was left of the evening destroyed by a private war being conducted around her. With a sigh, she stood. "Shall we go, before these two come to blows?"

Richard looked at her for the first time since he had watched her descend the stairs. He longed to support and comfort her, but he dared not. With a bored air, he said, "Of course, my dear; whatever you wish," and strolled to the door.

Diana whispered a goodbye to Edward and walked out the door, her chin in the air and her eyes filled with tears.

CHAPTER ELEVEN

DIANA DISREGARDED the rules of deportment and slumped in her chair at the breakfast table. She should have remained abed after the difficult evening spent at the Larrabys', but rest seemed impossible. She had awakened early, trying to understand her husband's behaviour.

Clare and Robert had remained at odds with each other the entire evening. Robert turned his attention to Diana, much to everyone's discomfort, and that had only increased Clare's anger, making Diana terribly uncomfortable. Richard, instead of supporting his old friend, had grown quieter as the evening progressed, but his eyes had flashed fire every time Diana spoke to him.

Boswell entered the breakfast parlour bearing a silver tray piled high with letters and invitations. He set the tray down beside his mistress and picked up the teapot to refill her cup. "May I bring you anything else, my lady?"

"No, thank you, Boswell." After the butler left the room, Diana sat in gloomy silence, occasionally sipping her tea. Finally, she began opening the post. Over a month was left of the Season and already she was tired of it. She sighed as she piled up the invitations.

Her husband's return had certainly increased their popularity.

Her mind on last night's outing, Diana opened another envelope, the unfamiliar feel of the rough, smudged paper at first escaping her notice. Only when she read the poorly printed words did she awaken from her thoughts. "If yer not kereful, ye'll die. Mad Molly."

With a gasp, Diana stared at the startling message. Very gently, she laid it on the table. After continuing to stare at it for several minutes, she reached with shaking fingers for her cup of tea. The cooling liquid revived her and she set down the cup to pick up the paper again. Drawing a deep breath, Diana studied the slanted words. What did the author intend? She picked up the envelope and looked at the name scrawled upon it: "Capt. Lord Rossley."

Richard! The threat was against Richard. Diana fought back the urge to rush up the stairs and see for herself that he was safe. Taking deep breaths, she steadied her heart.

Boswell opened the door to see if his mistress required his services. There was an unhappy air about her this morning that concerned him. Hoping to see uplifted spirits, he froze at his mistress's stricken look and pasty white cheeks. "My lady, what is amiss?" he gasped as he rushed to the table.

Startled, Diana let the envelope slip from her cold fingers and Boswell bent to pick it up.

"Boswell, have . . . have there been other letters addressed to Lord Rossley like this one?"

The butler studied the ill-formed hand on the dirty paper. "No, my lady. Is it bad news?"

"I—I—no. But I want you to watch for any other letters like this and...and give them to me, not to Lord Rossley. Will you do that?"

"If that is your wish, my lady," the man said slowly, his eyes on the envelope.

"Yes. Yes, it is my wish."

"My lady, if there is any difficulty, Lord Rossley could—"

"No! No, we mustn't bother Lord Rossley."

When his mistress said nothing else, Boswell turned to go, his expression reflecting his concern about what might have been in the letter.

"Boswell, wait. Do we have several large footmen?" When she realized the butler was staring at her in surprise, she said, "I mean, well, footmen who would be able to...to protect someone?"

"Of course, my lady. Who might they need to protect?"

"Lord Rossley."

"Protect him from what, my lady?"

Diana reluctantly placed the note in Boswell's hand. "I don't really know."

The butler read the brief note. "My lady, I think Lord Rossley should be informed of this threat."

"He will simply dismiss it as nonsense, Boswell."

He looked helplessly at his mistress.

Diana stared into space, frantically trying to determine her best path. "But he might take a little more care. Yes, you are right, Boswell. I shall place the message back in the envelope and say nothing to him, but we shall see that a footman follows him everywhere.''

''Will he not notice, my lady?'' Boswell asked, imagining his master's rage if he discovered that his household was following his every step.

''I do not think so. But you may rest assured that I will take full blame if he does.'' She paused, wondering how effective her plan would be. ''And, Boswell, you must watch the post and let me read any more missives like this one before Lord Rossley.''

''Yes, my lady.''

''Good morning,'' Lord Rossley said as he entered the dining room. ''Boswell, would you bring a fresh pot of tea?''

Fortunately, Lord Rossley did not notice Boswell's start or Diana's flush at his appearance. He filled a plate at the sideboard and sat down at the table, waiting for his tea.

''Good morning,'' Diana said with a quavery smile.

Richard looked at his wife for the first time that morning. ''Are you feeling quite the thing this morning, my lady?''

His cold tones reduced the concern in his words to nothing. ''Yes, I am very well,'' Diana said stiffly.

He only nodded and sampled a scone. Boswell entered and poured him a cup of steaming tea. ''My lady?'' he asked.

Diana almost said no, planning to leave her husband's presence as soon as possible. But a recollection of her plans made her acquiesce to another cup of tea.

"Do you have plans for today?" she asked in an attempt to appear unconcerned.

Lord Rossley lifted his head to stare at his wife. He had decided this morning that it mattered not to him if his wife was attracted to his best friend. After all, he didn't care for the woman—only for his reputation.

Now as he stared into his wife's large grey eyes, he felt a definite twinge in the heart. Fighting to remain untouched by her femininity, he said brusquely, "Of course."

Such rejection made continuing more difficult, but Diana ploughed on. "I wondered if you'd care to accompany me to call on Sara today. We shall probably not be able to see her, but I thought we should express our concern by leaving a card."

"All right," he agreed, unable to think of a reason not to.

"And perhaps a drive in the Park afterwards?"

"Are you hoping to encounter Robert there?" he growled, surprised by her request.

"Robert? In the Park? I do not believe he goes there often," Diana said, puzzled.

Richard only grunted and continued eating.

"Why did you think I was looking for Robert? We spent the evening with him last night."

"You do not need to inform me of that. He was in your pocket the entire evening."

"Only because he and Clare were at odds," Diana assured him, relieved to have the conversation turn to a more comfortable subject. When Richard made no response, Diana asked, "You have no objection to the connection, do you?"

"I have no objection."

"Surely you don't think Edward would object?" Diana didn't think it possible, but Richard seemed to be implying that someone would not care for the match.

"No."

His abrupt answer left Diana uneasy. "Richard, whatever is the matter?"

"I saw you and Robert in the drawing-room on Thursday evening. It was obvious you were...sharing secrets."

Diana surprised her husband by chuckling. "Well, not precisely secrets. It seems all of us are aware of Clare and Robert's romance."

"And last evening? You expect me to believe you kept Robert at your side only because Clare was angry?"

"What other reason could there— Richard! You surely do not believe—how could you?" Diana demanded, rising from her chair.

The pain in Diana's voice convinced Richard more than any rational argument that he had made a fatal error. "My lady, calm yourself. It merely seemed..."

Diana backed away from the table, her eyes never leaving her husband. In a low voice, she said, "I had such hopes upon your return. I wanted a real family, happiness. I worked so hard to remain faithful to my vows, even when I did not know you. And now I am repaid with your absurd suspicions."

"If they are untrue, my lady, I—"

"*If?* My lord, they are so unfounded they are ridiculous!"

She turned to go, tears in her eyes.

"Wait!" Richard commanded.

"For what? So you may address me as 'my lady'? You cannot even bear to say my name. There is nothing to wait for!"

In spite of his order to stay, she departed at once. Richard, now standing, sank slowly to his chair. Had he made a horrible mistake? He had only described what he had seen, he told himself in justification. If she did not want to be accused of improprieties, she should ensure that her behaviour was proper.

He took a bite of a tasteless scone. Her behaviour was proper; he had to admit that. Certainly, her being closeted with Robert was not quite *comme il faut,* but they were old friends. The scone fell from his hands unnoticed.

Diana. He *could* say her name. In fact, he took pleasure in saying it as it called to mind her grey eyes, warm and intelligent, her slim body which had fitted so perfectly against his in the drawing-room when he comforted her. It was for that very reason that he tried to avoid her name. He didn't *want* to have any feelings for her, to worry about her faithfulness, to want her.

He jumped up and strode from the room. Damn! Life was growing too difficult. It had been easier fighting Boney's army.

DIANA SAT UP and wiped her cheeks dry. She would not cry for what might have been. She had learned that lesson, at least, more than a year ago. The lesson she had not learned was how to protect her heart from the pain of loving.

He thought she would betray him as his first wife had done. That lack of faith hurt, but she should have expected it. Well, she must continue on as before, doing what she believed best. The dreams she had allowed to grow after Richard's return must be put away.

It was time to count her blessings, starting with Melly. And she must visit the child right away or she would be wondering if her mama had forgot her. She straightened her hair and washed her face with cool water. As for Richard, she would put him from her mind.

Only as she started up the stairs to the third floor did she remember the need to protect her husband. She sent one of the tweenies dusting in the hallway to Boswell to remind him to have a footman "accompany" his lordship when he went out.

SEVERAL HOURS LATER, Richard, dressed for an outing, descended to the first floor and rang for Boswell. "Please send one of the maids up to see if her ladyship is ready to accompany me to visit Mrs. White."

While he knew Boswell might think his behaviour strange, Richard did not feel brave enough to face Diana himself at the moment. The relief he felt when she finally joined him was best not examined too closely.

"Are you ready...Diana," he said, struggling to say her name calmly.

Not looking at him, she responded, "Yes, my lord."

He bit his bottom lip and said nothing. If her formality was the only price he paid for his disbelief, he would be lucky. "Very well. The carriage is waiting."

"One moment, please. I—I wondered if you'd mind if a footman accompanied us in place of your tiger today." Because he was still unable to use his left hand sufficiently to handle a team, and was therefore unable to drive his curricle himself, Jeb, his coachman, drove Lord Rossley in the barouche. His tiger, eager to serve his lordship, had begun riding up behind him in the barouche, ready to run errands.

"For what reason?"

Without looking at him, she said, "I—I intend to do some shopping after our visit, and I do not want to delay you from your appointments. I thought the footman could accompany me and carry the packages."

Her reasoning seemed logical and he did not want to upset her again, so he agreed. Only when they reached the bottom of the steps did he wonder if he should reconsider. There, standing behind the seat, instead of the diminutive figure of his tiger, whose head barely topped his own when he was seated, was the largest of their footmen. He was a huge giant of a man, used in the household for the heaviest chores.

"Er, Diana, must you take Lester? Surely you are not planning to purchase such heavy items? They may be sent to the house."

"You object to Lester?" Diana asked coolly.

Wary of offending her, Richard only said, "He looks like a great oak, standing up behind us." In his green livery, Lester did resemble a shade tree more than a tiger.

"I prefer Lester," she said firmly, lifting a hand to Richard for assistance in seating herself in the carriage.

"Very well," he muttered, giving the footman a frowning glance.

The stares their short drive drew told Richard he was not the only one to think Lester a bizarre choice for his position, but he said nothing. Once they reached the Whites' house, he put the man from his mind.

As the butler opened the door to the parlour to announce them, angry voices drifted out.

"I do not care to be considered a responsibility! Especially *your* responsibility!"

"Well, you are! You have always been, ever since I met you!" Robert roared back at the delicate female, dressed in soft pink muslin, her curls hanging in perfect spirals. The porcelain prettiness of her face was dispelled by the angry sparks in her eyes.

"I shall not— Oh! Diana, Richard, I did not hear the butler—"

"I am afraid we followed too closely on his heels, Clare. How…how is everything today?" Diana asked, her gaze dashing back and forth between the two combatants.

"Fine," Clare said stiffly, turning her back on Robert.

"And Sara?"

"Oh, she is much more the thing. She says she feels a fraud staying in bed, but Edward insists. Would you like to go up and visit her?"

"If you do not think it would be too tiring."

"No, she would enjoy the diversion." Clare turned to lead the way, ignoring the male audience.

"Is Edward here?" Richard asked.

"Sir Robert is awaiting my brother-in-law. I'm sure he'll be down soon." With her nose in the air, Clare swept from the room, taking Diana with her.

"Well, that is an invigorating way to start the day, Robert," Richard said with a slight smile.

"Why not? I seem to be at odds with everyone these days," he responded with a pointed look at his friend.

"I, er, I owe you an apology for last evening, and the evening of our entertainment also. I will admit to feeling unreasonable jealousy when Diana centred her attentions on you."

"You still have that bee in your bonnet, do you?" Robert growled.

"Not any longer. I was wrong to distrust her, Robert, and I'm asking you to forget my regrettable behaviour." Richard extended his hand hopefully.

With a slanted grin, Robert accepted his apology. "Of course, Richard. Females! They'll drive us all mad."

"I think you may be right. You and Clare are—"

"At each other's throats. I don't understand what is wrong with the chit. Edward is my friend. Of course I must assist him in his responsibilities when there are difficulties."

"I think she seeks more than responsibility from you."

"That is just her infatuation. She will outgrow it. All women are the same when a soldier comes home from the war."

"Oh? I'm told she rejected Major Tomlinson just last week," Richard said casually, but his eyes watched his friend closely.

"Teddy Tomlinson? He's a fine man, good fortune."

"Yes, an excellent catch for any young woman—a hero, in fact."

Robert frowned and began pacing the floor. The door opened to reveal Edward. "Good morning."

"Hello, Edward. I understand Sara is in better frame this morning?"

"Yes, thank you, Richard. She is much better. Can you believe it? She had made up her mind that I did not care for her anymore because I was spending so much time with you two." He grinned. "I soon put such foolish notions to the rout."

"Good for you," Richard said, wishing he were as adept at handling his own wife.

"Did Clare really reject Tomlinson last week?" Robert blurted out.

"Well, just between us, yes, she did. But that shouldn't be bruited about," Edward said.

"Why?"

Such a bald question surprised Edward. He shrugged and said, "She only said she could not care for him."

"He is handsome, has a pretty fortune, is a hero from the war," Robert insisted.

"Yes."

"Didn't you point out those things to her?"

"Rob, what is the point? Clare knows all those things. She is able to make her own decisions. Her mother and Sara both assured me I should give her her head."

"That's not the way it is supposed to be done, Edward."

"If you think you can do better with a beautiful, headstrong young woman whose only parent lets her determine her own way, I wish you well with her. I'll gladly turn over my authority, what little I have." When Robert said nothing, Edward prodded, "Well, Robert? Are you offering for Clare?"

"Don't be ridiculous! I am a cripple and Clare is a diamond of the first water. We don't belong together."

"For a cripple, you are certainly doing your best to wear out Edward's Aubusson carpet," Richard said mildly.

Robert paused in his pacing. With a rueful grin, he said, "My leg is growing stronger, but I shall always limp."

"That don't seem to bother Clare," Edward reminded him. "She even waltzed with you, as I recall."

The two ladies returned to the parlour at that moment, making a further discussion of Clare's fate impossible. Both ladies remained by the door and

Richard noted with suspicion that Clare, as well as Diana, had on her outer garments.

"Edward, Diana and I are going shopping, if you do not mind. Sara would like some wool so she may begin making things for the baby."

"Of course, my dear. You are taking a maid with you?"

As Clare nodded and the two women turned to go, Richard stopped them. "You have Lester, Diana. There is no need to take one of Edward's maids as well."

Diana avoided his eyes, a sure sign to Richard that she was being less than honest. "It seems that Lester injured his ankle yesterday and would have difficulty walking, so I think it best if he remain with you."

In addition to his suspicions, the picture of himself parading through the Park with a coachman up front and the huge footman hulking over him made Richard protest. "Lester should not be on his feet if he has injured himself. I'll have Jeb take him home."

"No! No, he hates being cooped up. A drive would be a treat for him."

Now he was sure Diana was plotting something, but he could not imagine what. However, he only nodded, certain he would get nothing else out of her. The two women left the room.

"Well, Edward, would you care to accompany us to Watier's?" Richard asked, assuming Robert would be coming with him.

"No, I must stay here with Sara. She is uneasy if I am away too long." With a happy smile on his face, he showed his two friends to the door.

"He seems quite pleased to be confined to quarters with his wife," Robert said slowly as they descended the front steps.

"If it were Clare carrying your child, would you not also want to protect and care for her?" Richard asked, his mind putting Diana in Sara's place and discovering a surge of warmth in his body.

"By God, yes, of course, but that is out of the— Richard, is that Lester?" Robert asked, awestruck as he noticed the footman standing at the heads of Richard's horses.

"Yes," Richard replied grimly, his mind brought back to the little mystery his wife had presented him.

"His feet would hit the ground if he were astride one of your horses. We could have used him on the Continent."

With an absent-minded response, Richard strolled over to the waiting footman. "I'm sorry to hear you injured your ankle, Lester. Just how did it happen?"

The big man stared down at his master, puzzled. "What, my lord?"

"Do you mean to say you did not injure your ankle?"

"No, my lord. I couldn't walk if I'd done that, could I?"

Richard stroked the forehead of one of his bays as he asked, "Who told you to accompany us this morning?"

"Mr. Boswell."

"Just what did he say you were to do?"

Lester turned red and ran his finger round his collar as if it were too tight. "I—I'm not supposed to tell you, your lordship."

"Am I your employer, Lester?" Richard asked gently. At the large man's nod, Richard said, "Then I command you to tell me what Boswell said to you."

"H-he said I was to keep close to your lordship and protect you from everyone."

Richard and Robert exchanged startled glances. "Protect me? From what?" Richard demanded.

"I don't rightly know, my lord. I just do what Mr. Boswell tells me. He gets right starchy if I ask questions."

"If you do not mind, Robert, I think we shall return to my household and discover the meaning of this conspiracy before we go to Watier's."

Robert nodded as he followed Richard into the carriage. "I agree. Has someone threatened you?"

After instructing his coachman, Richard replied, "Not that I know of."

They travelled the short distance to the Rossley house in silence. Each had much to think about. When they disembarked at the steps, Richard commanded Lester to follow him as his tiger, who had been jealously waiting for his master's return, eagerly took the horses.

Boswell's eyes widened at the sight of Lord Rossley and Sir Robert entering the house, Lester following in their wake. He was even more alarmed when his master signalled he wished both Lester and Boswell to follow them into the parlour.

"Yes, my lord? Would you be wishing a tea tray?" Boswell asked, in an attempt to delay the inevitable.

"I do not think that will be necessary. Please pull the door to behind you."

Boswell did so, shooting a fulminating glance at his underling.

"No, no, Boswell. You must not scold Lester. After all, he only did what his employer bade him do. Is that not right, Lester?"

The big man nodded eagerly, slanting a glance at the butler.

"Just as I'm sure *you* always do, Boswell. I have never had reason to find fault with your conduct or your loyalty before now."

Alarm spread on the old man's face, and Richard regretted his words. "Remain claim, Boswell. I only want to know why Lester was assigned to protect me. And from what?"

The old man's face turned red and he moved his lips several times, but no sound came out.

"Let me guess," Richard said. "You promised you would not tell?"

Boswell nodded fiercely.

Robert watched in amusement. As a commander of his men, Richard was known for his kindness, but he always expected obedience. He would expect no less in his household.

"I cannot think who could command your loyalty more than me, Boswell," Richard said, an injured look on his features. When the butler said nothing, he added softly, "Unless it is her ladyship."

CHAPTER TWELVE

Boswell's cheeks paled under his master's stare. "Her ladyship only wanted to protect you, my lord."

Richard frowned. "From what must I be protected?"

"The letter in your post, my lord. Lady Rossley showed it to me."

"Where is the letter?"

"In the study, my lord, with the rest of the post." Boswell breathed a sigh of relief when his master strode past him with no more questions. His relief disappeared when Lord Rossley called over his shoulder, "Both of you follow me."

Boswell and Lester fell in after Sir Robert and the four men entered the study. Lord Rossley shuffled through the large stack of bills and invitations until he came to the dingy envelope which had so affected his wife. He read the brief message several times and then showed it to the waiting Robert.

"Does this make sense to you?" he asked his friend.

"Well, I've heard of Mad Molly. Her husband was killed on the Continent. She came to the War Office once and offered her services."

"And?"

Sir Robert shrugged. "She has supplied them with bits of information. Last year she was instrumental in stopping a shipment of guns headed for Napoleon's men. Less than four months ago, I was told, confidentially of course, that a spy was arrested. There'd been no suspicion of the man until Mad Molly observed several private meetings between him and a Frenchman of ill repute."

Richard stared across the room, distracted. Then he turned to his friend. "Where is she to be found?"

"Down in the mud-flats along the Thames," Robert said, naming the worst area in the city. It was the den of thieves and murderers. Even brawny Lester shuddered to think of such a place.

"Lester, have you ever visited the area?"

His eyes grew large as Lester shook his head. "I never gone there, my lord."

"If you took along several well-armed companions, would you do so for me?"

With a gulp, Lester straightened his shoulders. "If'n that's what you want, your lordship."

"What do you intend?" Robert asked with a frown.

"I'm wondering if this woman knows of our efforts because of our grooms. We should have realized even they would be out of their element in such seedy surroundings. I am hoping the woman is warning us that others are aware of our interest and has heard of threats. Perhaps this Mad Molly might even be willing to help us." He turned to his servant. "Lester, I would like you to deliver a message to the woman for me. And gather up a goodly supply of food and—" he paused, digging into his pocket and pulling up some coins "—and this money to take to her also. Her life cannot be an easy one."

"Yes, my lord."

"Boswell, please ensure that Lester has several like-sized men with arms to accompany him. I do not want him to suffer for his loyalty."

The relief on Lester's face brought a lopsided smile to Richard's, and he extended his hand to his servant. Lester stared at the rare gesture and then offered his own with a blush.

"Thank you, Lester."

The man gulped and nodded.

Richard turned to Boswell. "Is Lady Rossley dining at home this evening?"

"Yes, my lord."

"I shall be joining her, Boswell, and I shall reassure her there is no need for any protection." He paused before adding, "I commend you and Lester for your loyalty to her ladyship."

After Boswell's grateful acknowledgement of his words, Richard dismissed the two men.

Robert asked, "What are you planning? I've seen that look in your eye before."

Richard grinned but shook his head. "I am planning nothing. I was just contemplating my conversation with my wife this evening."

"You would not hold her actions against her?" Robert asked sternly, his amusement gone.

With a glare, Richard said, "I would remind you that my dealings with my wife are private."

"Surely you are not still under the delusion that there is any—that Diana—"

"No, but I have no more desire to discuss Diana with you than you have to discuss Clare with me," he snapped.

Before Robert could speak, his frown undiminished, Richard tactfully turned the subject. "We must resemble mad dogs, growling at each other. I apologize, Robert. Shall we go to Watier's now, our original destination?"

"Yes, of course," Robert said in relief. "I seem to have grown testy of late."

Friends again, the two left the house and headed for their club, the war once more uppermost in their minds.

RICHARD PACED THE FLOOR in the parlour, waiting for Diana to descend for dinner. He had thought of speaking to her about her fears when she returned from shopping, but she only returned when he was already preparing for their evening.

After dinner, they were supposed to attend several parties, escorting Clare, of course. Sara was still keeping to her bed. The only opportunity he would have to talk to Diana alone was at dinner, and they would have to dine hurriedly now, late as it was.

Boswell stepped into the room. "My lord, her ladyship requests you to excuse her from dinner. She is dining on a tray in her room in order to prepare for the evening."

"Very well, Boswell. I will dine at once," he said in reserved tones. As he followed the butler into the dining room, his thoughts were not as restrained. Damn! Now he would have no time to reassure her of his safety. Or to warn her about attempting to take things into her own hands. After all, he was the head of his household.

After a lonely meal, he waited at the bottom of the stairs. He had begun to think her return had been a hoax when a slight movement drew his attention to the top of the stairs. Diana, Lady Rossley, was descending the stairs in a royal blue silk gown, its puffed sleeves and low décolleté revealing a great deal of her shoulders and bosom. Diamonds glittered at her ears and throat and long gloves covered her hands and arms. There was a flush in her pale cheeks and her grey eyes glowed.

Richard stood mesmerized by her appearance. With a flick of her wrist, she opened a hand-painted silk fan and swept him a curtsy. "I apologize for my tardiness, my lord."

"It is naught," he said, his gaze never leaving her.

"Shall we go?" she prompted when he did not move.

"Oh. Yes." He extended his arm and she lightly laid her fingers upon it.

They were halfway to Edward's before he remembered he had wanted to speak to her about the letter. He cleared his throat, finding himself ill at ease with the glittering beauty across from him. "Madam, I would—"

He regretted his form of address when he saw her stiffen, her face frozen in distaste.

"I apologize—that is, I forgot—Diana," he finally said, now thoroughly rattled. "I would ask that you not keep secrets from me in the future."

"I beg your pardon, my lord," she icily replied, assuming he spoke of Sara's pregnancy. "I did not realize *you* kept no secrets."

"That has nothing to do with—"

"It has everything to do with it, my lord." She turned to stare out the small window, ignoring the fuming man sitting opposite her.

Richard drew a deep breath. He had better think before he said anything else. The woman was touchy this evening, and he had not got off to a good beginning.

"Diana..." he began, but the halting of the carriage and the immediate opening of the door made continuing impossible.

Half an hour later, they were on their way again, but Clare sat beside Diana and the two women chatted about their shopping expedition all the way to the first party.

All evening Richard was lionized wherever they went. He avoided the dance floor, pleading his indisposition as his excuse when debutantes sought him out, wanting the social approval of the latest hero. Needless to say, Diana made no attempt to entice him into a dance. Barely half a dozen words were spoken between them the entire evening.

Finally, he allowed himself to be drawn into a card-game. He had only been at play for half an hour when a note was delivered to him by a footman.

My lord, Clare and I are tired and have prevailed upon Lord Anthony to escort us home. I shall have the carriage return for you.

Lady Rossley

It had not been his idea to attend the damn parties! Richard's face was grim as he nodded to the footman and extended a coin for his trouble. She had chosen Lord Anthony only to irritate him, he knew, and the formal signature on the the note was the last straw. He stood up from the table, his mind on the beautiful woman he'd watched come down the stairs, and walked away from those at the table without a word.

He was surprised to discover his carriage had already returned from its trip. When he questioned the coachman, he was informed her ladyship had travelled in Lord Anthony's coach. Almost exploding with anger, Richard climbed into the coach and came nigh to knocking the door off with a hard slam.

The warm feelings her concern had engendered were swept away in the flame of his rage. It was time his wife learned some rules of deportment.

KNOWING HER HUSBAND might not be pleased with her early departure the night before, Diana had intended to keep to her room the next day until it was time to pay calls. However, an early visitor brought her downstairs not long after she had finished both her toilette and the breakfast brought to her room.

"Hetta. How nice of you to call."

"Oh, my darling girl, I cannot thank you enough. I don't know how you convinced him, but I received my invitation this morning, and I could not wait to thank you. I never thought he would actually invite me to his house."

"Hetta, you must not—that is—"

"Good morning," Richard said from the door. He had asked Dawson to alert him when Lady Rossley came downstairs. His valet had scurried to his study with the news only a minute before, but he had neglected to mention who had called on Lady Rossley.

Hetta, sure all had been forgiven, leapt to her feet and flew across the room to Richard. "Oh, my dear boy, I am so grateful you have forgiven me at last! I swear I thought the two of you would be happy. I had no idea the child would...would behave as she did."

Her blue eyes filled with tears and Hetta whisked out a lacy handkerchief to collect the drops. "My heart has cried out for you, as I'm crying now," she continued dramatically. "But at last we can be a family once more."

She spun round to gesture towards Diana. "Such a lovely girl to take my Alicia's place. She loves Melly as much as I and she has pleaded my cause. Oh, Richard, I am so happy!" With a squeal of excitement, the small blond woman threw herself into Richard's arms and clung for dear life. Startled, he looked at Diana.

Pleading with her eyes for him to be kind, Diana held her breath as he stared at her. She watched as, with a grimace, he put some distance between his mother-in-law and himself.

"Control yourself, Hetta. If—" he paused and looked at Diana for a long moment "—if we are to be a family, you must give up some of your play-acting."

Hetta caught his hand and carried it to her cheek. "Oh, Richard," she said with a watery chuckle. "You are the drollest man, and the kindest, too."

"And you must promise to do as Diana asks in regard to Melly. I won't have her spoiled as you spoiled Alicia."

Tears of remorse replaced those of joy in Hetta's eyes. "Truly, Richard, I did not realize—I only wanted her to make a good marriage. I had followed my heart and lived too many penniless years regretting it. And you must admit she was beautiful," the woman pleaded, hoping for some sort of forgiveness.

Again Richard looked at his wife before answering. "Yes, Hetta, she was beautiful. As Melly will be. But we must be sure she has a more sensible head on her shoulders—like her new mama."

"Yes, of course," Hetta agreed in relief. "Diana combines beauty and wisdom. She is such a wonderful girl." She rushed back over to the couch to hug Diana.

As she received the embrace, Diana tried to thank her husband with her eyes. He looked at her but kept his features blank.

"I assume you are responding affirmatively to our invitation, Hetta?" Diana asked, teasing.

"You silly child! Of course I am. I would not stay away even if Prinny himself requested my presence."

She settled herself on the sofa beside Diana and took up the social prattle that she was prone to repeat. Much to Diana's surprise, Richard settled in a chair across from them and listened to the woman's chatter.

When Hetta Chadwell rose to leave, Diana accompanied her to the door. Richard followed when it appeared Diana had no intention of returning to the parlour.

"Lady Rossley," he called, halting her ascent up the stairs.

"Yes, my lord?"

"I would have a word with you, please, in the study."

"Could it not wait? I promised Melly I would take her for a ride in the Park."

"I will not take much of your time. Melly must be patient."

Robbed of her only excuse, Diana came slowly down the stairs.

Her reluctance to be closeted with him even for a moment put his back up. He stiffly motioned for her to precede him. Though she sat down in one of the chairs across from his desk, he chose to remain standing.

After a silence during which Diana kept her gaze trained on her hands, Richard cleared his throat and asked, "What are your plans for this evening?"

Diana, who had expected a scolding because of Hetta, Lester or her early return the previous evening, looked up at him, her lips quivering with laughter. "That is why you wanted to speak to me?"

"It is not the only reason," Richard replied, his lips tightening at her laughter. "I wanted to assure you I'll make myself available, since you have agreed to escort Clare." He paused before adding in harsh tones, "And *I* will escort you home."

Diana decided to ignore the implication of his words. "That is most kind of you, my lord. I believe we are to attend the Lancaster ball this evening."

"I know you are pretending to misunderstand me, madam, but I insist—"

"Madam?" Diana queried coolly.

"You are trying to distract me. I will not have you going home with Lord Anthony."

"I was escorted to *my* home by Lord Anthony, my lord. If you are not careful, you will start new rumours." Diana watched her husband's face redden with anger and regretted giving in to her sense of humour. "If you will think, my lord, I am only doing you a favour," she hurriedly added, hoping to ease the tension.

"You are doing me a favour by taking up with another man?" Lord Rossley growled.

"Of course. If we are always seen together, Society will think you are in love with your wife, which is most unfashionable. They would expect you always to live in my pocket, and I know you would not approve of that.''

Her peace-making efforts did not succeed. Richard, thoroughly incensed, though he did not understand why, pulled her from her chair and into his arms. ''Better for me to be in your pocket than to be cuckolded again.''

Diana stared up into his icy blue eyes and wished once more that her husband could at least trust her, even if love was an impossibility.

''Have you nothing to say, my lady?'' He watched her face intently, but his entire body was aware of her warmth pressed against him. Desire rose even as he fought it off.

Diana lowered her eyes, her limbs beginning to tremble because of their embrace. ''I have no desire to betray you . . . Richard,'' she whispered.

He lifted her face to his. ''I would believe you, my lady, if experience had not taught me better. But I will not allow poachers to take what is mine.''

Fire stirred in Diana's grey eyes. ''Is that all I am? A possession to be used at your convenience and discarded? Never to be touched by either you or others?''

Richard's fingers stroked her cheek as he said, ''You are mine by law, and no one else may touch you. But you are not in the least convenient, my lady.'' His last words came out in a whisper as his head bent and his lips took hers.

Diana had ached for a renewal of his caress, and she did not draw back from him. Her arms slid up about his neck and she acceded to the pressure of his arms.

Lost in their embrace, neither one heard the discreet knock at the door, nor the door opening. Only when Lady Melanie, amazed at finding her parents embracing, squealed and called to them were they aware of their audience.

Springing apart, their faces flushed, Richard and Diana looked everywhere but at each other.

"I'm sorry, my lady, but Lady Melanie was ready to accompany you and I thought—"

"That's perfectly all right, Nanny," Diana assured the beaming old woman hurriedly. "I'll—I'll just go and fetch my things and we'll be on our way."

"Are you going to come with us, Papa?" Melly demanded, and Diana paused just outside the door to hear his answer.

"No, my pet, I cannot go with you today. I have an appointment."

Breathing a sigh of relief, Diana rushed up the stairs. She needed time to consider the morning's events, and it was impossible to think if Richard was near her.

"DAMN!" Richard muttered to himself after the door closed behind Lady Melanie and her nurse. He hadn't intended to kiss Diana, but he was finding it more and more difficult to remain aloof in her presence.

Perhaps he should take a mistress. In his youth he had done so, but the idealism with which he had entered his first marriage had caused him to reward the woman for her services and send her on her way. Afterwards, the bitterness which filled him had precluded even that kind of relationship. But since his return, certain needs were making themselves felt.

It was Diana's fault, of course. Not only was she attractive, but she also was gentle, soft, feminine, all that was kind.... His thoughts returned to those few moments when he had held her in his arms.

Yes, it was definitely Diana's fault. If she did not obtrude so into his life, he might not find her occupying his thoughts... his desires.

Selecting a mistress was bothersome, however. A sudden thought struck Lord Rossley. Why should he pay for a mistress when he had a perfectly good wife in his own house? After all, she had not resisted his kisses. In fact, if his judgement was not clouded by his own desires, she seemed to welcome his caresses. He banished that thought at once as it aroused longings he was not yet ready to deal with.

The only difficulty would be ensuring himself against pain. He must not allow his emotions to play a role in this relationship. He would not allow himself to care about the woman, but there was no reason why she should not fulfill her role as his wife.

The rest of the morning he found himself distracted by thoughts of his marriage. He pictured his wife's slim figure, dwelling lovingly on each curve, taking delicious pleasure in his thoughts. Only when his mind's eye inevitably encountered those serene grey eyes was there a shadow cast on his plans.

Even that was dismissed when thoughts of a son entered his mind. After all, they both had a duty to produce an heir for the title. Every lady knew that as her duty. He would enjoy a son, or two...and Melly needed brothers or sisters.

If their assignment for Lord Wyckham was resolved today, as he hoped it would be, he would have more time to devote to convincing his wife to agree to his plans. He had received an answer from Mad Molly early that morning, requesting them to meet her at an inn by the Thames. If anyone knew of illegal activities regarding the French, it would be Mad Molly.

By the time Robert and Edward arrived to pick him up for their appointment at two o'clock, he had resolved all his difficulties except one: how to explain his decision to his wife.

CHAPTER THIRTEEN

DIANA RETURNED HOME that afternoon with a smile on her lips. Her spirits were high. If nothing else, her husband was attracted to her. It was a beginning.

As she sped Melly up the stairs into the care of one of the maids, her spirits were dampened somewhat. A vision of Edward hovering over Sara, ensuring her every comfort, love filling his eyes, gave her pause. She knew that was what she really wanted: Richard's love.

Shoving such ridiculous desires away, Diana clung to her optimism. At least he was attracted to her.

"Has his lordship returned?" she asked of Boswell.

"No, my lady."

"Very well. I believe I shall go through the post since I didn't have time this morning. Is it in the study?"

"Yes, my lady."

"Bring me a tea tray there, then, Boswell. I vow I am prodigiously thirsty."

Diana sent her outer garments up the stairway with a maid and made her way to the study. As she entered, remembrance of her encounter with her husband only that morning swept over her, and it was several minutes before she turned her attention to the mail.

As Boswell brought in the tea tray, he remembered that another note had been delivered from Mad Molly. However, since his lordship had said he would inform her ladyship of the harmlessness of the notes, he dismissed the concern from his mind.

Diana discovered the note just after she had taken a reviving sip of hot tea. She left the remainder untouched.

"The Royal Goose, Tuesday, two o'clock. Mad Molly." Automatically verifying the hour on the mantel clock, Diana discovered it was already past three. Panic rolled over her, and she drew deep breaths to gain control over her emotions. Richard would not have been so foolish as to keep such an appointment. After all, the woman had threatened him with death in the last note. And even if he did, he would not have gone alone.

Jumping up from her chair, Diana paced the room. Even if she believed him to be in danger, what could she do? He became angry every time she interfered.

A surge of determination rose up in her. What did it matter if he was angry, as long as he was safe? Her dreams of happiness, of a family, of a dearly loved and loving husband were nothing compared to Richard's safety.

The pacing stopped and Diana sat down to decide on her best plan of action. Her only hope of not alienating Richard entirely was to effect his rescue with the minimum of fuss and without drawing the attention of others. Even Boswell would be better left in the dark.

A few minutes later, Boswell discovered his mistress in the foyer pulling on kid gloves, dressed for the out of doors.

"His lordship has not returned?" she asked.

Boswell searched her face for concern but saw nothing to worry him.

"No, my lady."

"Does he not usually return about now?" she asked as the clock struck four.

"Not always, my lady."

"Well, when he returns, please tell him I've gone out to do some shopping. Oh, is Lester available? Some of my packages may be heavy."

Boswell frowned. There was nothing he could object to, but a sense of uneasiness invaded him. "I'll send for him."

While she was awaiting Lester's arrival, Diana sought one more piece of information. "I assume Lord Rossley was accompanied by Sir Robert and Mr. White?"

The butler assured her he was. At that moment, Lester filled the doorway from the lower level of the house.

"Ah, Lester. Very well, we'll be on our way."

Their first stop was not one of the many shops on Bond Street, but the Whites' residence. As an old friend, Diana was shown into Sara's boudoir where she and Clare were chatting over their needlework.

Diana struggled to maintain her calm. She had foolishly alarmed Sara once before, and she did not want to do so again. At a pause in their conversation, she asked, "Did Edward say where he, Richard and Robert were going this afternoon, or when they would return?"

Sara frowned. "He said he had an appointment which he could not avoid, at two, I believe, but he promised to be back nearly an hour ago."

Diana laughed, though she feared the sound was unnaturally high. "Those three forget the time when they are together."

"Edward has been most faithful in his promises, particularly since he knows I am *enceinte,*" Sara protested.

Clare glared at her friend. "I'm sure he will return at any moment."

"Yes, of course. The traffic was unusually heavy this afternoon. My carriage scarcely moved at times."

Diana rose to her feet and smiled warmly at Sara. "And I must finish my errands if I am to return home at a reasonable hour myself." She turned to Clare and silently tried to convey her need to speak with her privately. "I will see you this evening," she said, her words accompanied by her eyebrows wiggling and her eyes blinking.

"Are you ill, Diana?" Clare asked, astonished.

"I believe I am not feeling quite the thing. Could you see me down the stairs, Clare?"

"You must lie down if you are unwell!" Sara exclaimed.

"No, no, I shall be fine. I just—"

"Clare, ring for some additional tea," Sara ordered.

"No, please, I am feeling much better," Diana insisted. "It was only a momentary weakness." She glared at Clare.

"I'll see Diana downstairs, Sara, just to be sure she is well," Clare finally said, staring strangely at their guest.

Diana bade a feeble adieu to Sara and left the room, followed by Clare. At the bottom of the stairs, she whispered, "I must be private with you."

Without comment, Clare led the way to the parlour. Once the door was closed, Diana said, "I wanted to leave word with you of my destination, should... should Richard—"

"What is the matter? Why didn't you just tell Boswell where—"

"I can't explain, Clare. I'm going to an inn named The Royal Goose. And do not tell Sara!" she added as she turned to go.

Clare's hand clamped down on her arm with surprising strength. "You must tell me the danger before you depart. Does it have something to do with...with Richard, Edward and Robert?"

"I cannot tell you. Just remember my destination in case... in case there is any difficulty," Diana said, attempting to pull free from Clare's grasp.

"No! Robert is in danger, isn't he? I won't let you go unless you tell me."

Diana stared at the fierce determination on her friend's face and capitulated. "Very well. But you must promise to tell no one."

She then explained about the threatening letter Richard had received and the second one in the post today setting a meeting place and time. "I believe he has gone to meet this person and... and I'm frightened. If Edward told Sara he would return over an hour ago, then something has delayed them. I must go and find them."

"What can you do alone?"

"I have Lester with me, and I took the pair of duelling pistols Richard keeps in his study. I loaded them and I'm going to carry one and give one to Lester. Jeb, our coachman, will stay with the carriage."

"I'm going with you," Clare stated firmly.

"No! You mustn't, Clare. I cannot be responsible for causing injury to someone else," Diana protested, pulling against Clare's hold.

"You will wait for me!" Clare insisted, her eyes hard with determination. "Do you think I value my life if Robert is in difficulties?"

"But, Clare—"

"Come with me. I'll get Edward's duelling pistols. I do not know how to load them but surely Lester or you can do that." Clare dragged her friend down the hall, resolution in her every step.

"But what about Sara? She is awaiting your return abovestairs," Diana reminded Clare as she struggled to keep her feet in the wake of her friend's march.

"I shall tell her they have just received a new shipment of the finest wool at one of the shops and I want
to have first selection."

Diana gave up trying to resist Clare's determination. Secretly, she was relieved not to go alone, but she
felt guilty at involving her friend.

Only a few minutes later, the intrepid pair emerged
from the house. Once they were seated in the carriage, Diana leaned forward. "Jeb, we need to visit an
inn called The Royal Goose. Do you know where it is
located?"

The grey-haired man scratched the back of his head
as he considered her request. "Must be a new one, my
lady, 'cause the only Royal Goose I've 'eard of is near
the mud-flats. Bad place to be located."

"No, Jeb, I believe that is the inn I am looking for.
Please take us to it."

"My lady, his lordship will 'ave my 'ead if'n I take
you to that place," the coachman protested.

"I will explain to him that I demanded you do so,"
Diana said calmly, holding her hands tightly together
to still their trembling.

Lester turned from his position beside the coachman. "My lady, Jeb is right. 'Tis not a safe part of
Town—for any of us."

Diana drew herself up stiffly and stared at the two
men in front of her. "Please take us to The Royal
Goose...*at once.*"

The men frowned at each other and turned round in
their seats, and the barouche moved forward. The two

young ladies leaned back against the cushioned seat, but neither was at ease.

"Do you think it is a terrible place?" Clare whispered.

"Would you arrange a meeting to harm someone in the best part of Town?" Diana demanded. "If you would like to remain at home, I will—"

"No! I will not remain behind when Robert—and the others—may be in danger."

Diana caught up Clare's hand and the two ladies gathered their courage together as they rode toward the worst neighbourhood in London.

RICHARD HANDED HIS HAT and cane over to Boswell with a sigh. Mad Molly's information had proved accurate about a certain shipment of goods. After a long afternoon of investigation tracing the owner, they had continued on to the War Office to inform Lord Wyckham.

It was disappointing to discover that the villain was one of those merchants who'd supped at his table. Sir Toby had warned him that the man was of questionable character, but he hadn't dreamed the man would be so greedy as to supply both armies, hoping to sustain a profitable war at the cost of men's lives.

He and his friends were relieved to be finished with their investigation. As a straightforward soldier, Richard found subterfuge not to his liking. Edward was now pleased to be able to turn his attention to his expectant wife, and Lord Rossley also had plans regarding *his* lady.

"I am grateful to be home, Boswell." As he started for the stairs, he asked, "Has her ladyship enquired after me?"

"Yes, my lord, and she said to tell you she had some late shopping to do."

Richard looked at the hall clock. Almost half-past five. "And she has not returned?"

"No, my lord."

"What time did she depart?"

"Near on four o'clock, my lord. And she took Lester with her."

Richard swung round sharply to stare at the butler. "Does she often take Lester with her?"

"Never, my lord, until the letter from Mad Molly."

Richard stood still in thought.

"Since you told her that the letters were no cause for concern, I knew it couldn't be on account of them..." the butler began.

"Well, as to that, Boswell, I haven't yet had an opportunity to discuss it with her ladyship, but I will—"

"But the letter!" said Boswell suddenly. "If she believes—"

"She found the second letter from Mad Molly?"

"It was in the library, my lord, when her ladyship said she'd look at the post. I didn't say anything because I thought you'd—"

"Damn! I forgot to destroy it. My brain must be going soft." He stood a moment with his head bent in thought. "You're sure she saw it?"

"I don't know, my lord. I removed the tea tray her ladyship requested, but she'd hardly touched the tea and didn't try Cook's special pastries at all. Most upset, Cook was."

Each word from the butler sounded more ominous than the one before. Since Diana had already been upset by the earlier note, he was afraid she might have placed the wrong interpretation upon the poorly scribbled words he had received early this morning. "Call her maid!" he snapped.

The butler hurried up the stairs, and Richard entered the library. The first thing to catch his eye was an open case on the library table. His eyes sharpened as he recognized the box that held his duelling pistols. Striding over, he found it empty.

"Yes, my lord?" Diana's maid asked, the butler towering behind her.

"Did her ladyship indicate where she was going this afternoon?"

"No, my lord," the woman said, trembling. "Be there anything wrong?"

"No. I simply hoped to join her," he said smoothly, his gaze going to Boswell in warning. "Thank you. You may go." He stood quietly until the woman had departed before turning back to the butler. "What time did you say she left?"

"About four, my lord."

"Mad Molly wanted to meet me at The Royal Goose at two this afternoon. Lady Rossley couldn't have gone to keep the appointment if she left that late. Where is she?"

"Perhaps she thought you kept the appointment and was concerned about your late return," Boswell suggested.

"But she would not have been foolish enough to venture near The Royal Goose. That is near the mudflats." Richard paced a few steps before he came to a conclusion. "She would have gone to Edward's first to see if we'd returned. Tell the groom to saddle my horse, Boswell, and be quick about it," he called as he ran out of the study and up the stairs.

With the small pistol he kept in his chamber in his pocket and additional funds, which often worked better than bullets in the poorer parts of London, Richard raced down the stairs, out the door and mounted his favourite stallion. The horse's restless spirit suited his master's, and they dashed through the crowded streets, narrowly avoiding collisions everywhere.

"Where is your master?" Richard demanded as he raced into Edward's house, having left his horse's reins in the hands of a footman.

"In the parlour, my lord, with Sir Robert."

Richard didn't wait to be announced, but threw open the door to the parlour. "Edward, is Diana here?"

"Here? No, she and Clare went out shopping."

Richard came to an abrupt halt. "Clare? Clare is with her?"

"Yes. What is the matter?" Edward asked, finally noting his friend's agitated state.

Richard shook his head, frowning. Would she have taken Clare into such danger? Of course not. He was being ridiculous...wasn't he?

Robert strolled over to Richard's side. "Have you misplaced your wife, old friend? You weren't suspecting me again, were you?"

His teasing drew no smile from Richard. "Did they say where they were going?"

Robert and Edward exchanged looks. "I will ask Sara," Edward said and left the room.

"What is it, Richard? Are you concerned about Diana?"

"I forgot to destroy the message from Mad Molly," Richard said. His cheeks flushed as he admitted, "I intended to explain about the letter to Diana but...but there's been no time. I'm afraid she found it and thought I needed assistance. She would not be so foolish as to go to The Royal Goose, would she, Robert?"

"What did she tell Boswell?"

"That she had late shopping to do. But she asked that Lester accompany her, and she has never done that before. And she left her tea tray untouched after requesting it." Richard gulped before he added, "And my duelling pistols are gone."

Robert groaned. "Surely she would not have...and she took Clare with her?" Without another word, Robert turned to run from the room.

"Where are you going?" Richard demanded.

"After them! You know how dangerous that part of Town is!"

"Of course I do. But let's wait until we hear from Edward. We could be jumping to conclusions."

"You know we are not. Ladies do not take duelling pistols on a shopping expedition," Robert insisted. "We are wasting time!"

Edward ended their argument. "They told Sara there was a new shipment of wool at a shop on Bond Street and they wanted to have first choice."

"Edward, do you have duelling pistols?" Robert asked.

"Yes, of course I do," Edward replied, bewildered. "What does that have to do with Diana and Clare?"

"Get them. We'll explain on the way," Robert insisted.

The two others followed Edward to a small back room where he kept his weapons. An empty case was all that remained.

"Aha! I was right," Robert said.

"They took mine, also," Richard assured the puzzled Edward. "We think the two ladies have gone to The Royal Goose."

"Don't be ridiculous! Why would they go there?"

"I'll explain as we ride. We have no time to waste. Do you have any other weapons?" Richard asked. "I only have a small pistol."

Edward took out additional firearms, giving one to each of his friends. Robert had requested horses to be saddled, and after a message had been sent up to Sara to explain his absence, Edward, Robert and Richard were soon riding in haste to The Royal Goose.

CHAPTER FOURTEEN

THE TWO YOUNG WOMEN clutched each other more and more tightly as they drove deeper into the misery of London. Soulless eyes stared at the elegant young ladies, such an unusual sight in the narrow, filthy streets.

"My lady, this ain't safe," Lester protested hoarsely at one point, but Diana, white-faced, insisted they go on. Finally, they reached the crumbling inn with the barely visible words The Royal Goose hanging over its door.

"Diana, I'm frightened," Clare whispered.

Diana stared warily at their destination. "Me too, Clare, but I cannot turn my back if Richard is in need of my assistance."

Men began to draw closer to the carriage, some hawking their miserable wares, others making remarks that Diana wasn't sure she understood, something for which she was grateful. "I wish we had left word with your butler where we were going," she muttered.

Clare moaned at the thought. "What do we do now?"

"Lester," Diana called softly, leaning towards the giant of a man.

"Yes, my lady?" he answered, though he never took his eyes from the crowd growing around them.

"Here," Diana said and reached out a hand holding a pistol. "It's loaded."

He took the gun and realized his mistress was extending still another one. "Give this to Jeb."

Diana swallowed before turning to Clare. "I'm going to take Lester and...and go inside. You stay here with Jeb to ensure the carriage is not overrun with...with these people."

"I can't let you go in there alone!"

"Lester will be with me. I think your presence will help Jeb. We cannot leave him here all alone." They stared at each other for what seemed like ages before Clare accepted her decision. Diana wasn't sure it was any safer in the carriage than inside the inn, but she hoped it was. She didn't want her friend hurt because of her.

"Very well, but...be careful, Diana."

Drawing a deep breath, Diana agreed to have a care and gestured for Lester to come with her. That worthy individual bravely followed his mistress, but he did not do so enthusiastically.

Jeb, left to tend the carriage with the other young lady in his care, said several prayers to be delivered from such a hell-hole with his passengers intact. If he left without them, he might as well remain, as it would undoubtedly be more peaceful than reporting their loss to his lordship.

Diana shuddered as the men closed in about her. Raising her chin, her pistol hidden beneath the folds of her skirt, she walked to the entrance of The Royal Goose, with Lester behind her.

It was almost dark outside already, but inside the inn only a feeble lantern and a small fire in the grate gave off light. Diana stood still, hoping her eyes would adjust.

Her presence, quickly noted by several men near the door, drew an unnerving silence. When all was quiet, she moved forward. Afraid no sound would come out, she cleared her throat and said, "I'm searching for Lord Rossley. Has he been here this afternoon?"

"And who might you be? His doxy?" a raw voice demanded, followed by others' laughter.

"I am Lady Rossley. Where is the innkeeper?" Her voice gathered strength as she spoke.

"I be 'ere," a greasy old man replied, helped forward by a boot from an ungrateful customer.

"Has a gentleman been here this afternoon, about two of the clock? Accompanied by two others?"

"I'se a gent. Will I do, pretty lady?" a bosky customer offered, shoving his way forward.

Even as Diana drew back in a mixture of fear and disgust, Lester shoved the man away, causing him to fall backwards across a table. His fall drew laughter from some, but others were quick to protest the arrogance of the gentry and their minions.

"Please, we do not mean you any harm," Diana pleaded, desperation moving her. "But I must find my husband. Someone...someone threatened him and—"

"''Ere now, ain't no one 'ere broke the law!'' the innkeeper protested, only to be met by more howling laughter.

"No, no, I'm accusing no one of— Don't!" she exclaimed as a man pulled on her skirts, the stench rising from him filling the air. Lester stepped forward to intervene and found himself attacked by several of the braver and less sober customers.

Diana didn't hesitate to reveal her pistol. She could not endanger Lester. "Halt!"

The sight of the pistol brought a sudden stillness to the room.

The innkeeper edged closer. "M'lady, no call to shoot anyone. There be no lord 'ere, nor 'as there ever been. Only we ordinary folk."

Diana, feeling the walls closing in around her as the leering men and the offending scent seemed to move closer, swung her pistol towards the man. "But he must have come. The note said The Royal Goose at two o'clock."

He backed off, his hands raised, one still holding a dirty rag. "I ain't seen no strangers 'ere."

She had been so sure Richard had come there. Now she didn't know what to do. Lester stood beside her, his pistol now drawn also, but the two of them could not effect a search. And she could not leave Clare and Jeb outside for very long.

"Why don't you sit a spell, little hell-cat. We don't often get females like you down 'ere."

Feeling the bile rise in her throat, Diana backed away from the outstretched hand of the man who had spoken. "Lester," she whispered, "I believe we should go."

"Yes, my lady," he said with relief.

But as the fashionable lady and the large footman began edging their way out the door, those inside decided they were not happy to see them go. Suddenly, Diana found the pistol knocked from her hand as she was dragged forward into their midst. Lester, his eyes on his mistress, was pounded from behind by a chair and crashed to the floor, dropping his pistol as he fell.

CLARE MOVED to the forward seat of the barouche, her back to the coachman. "Jeb?" she whispered.

"Yes, Miss Seaton?" he muttered in return, his eyes not leaving the people milling about his coach and horses.

"I have my back to you. I'll watch those behind us if you'll watch those in front."

"You have a pistol, Miss Seaton?" he asked hopefully.

"Yes. But I don't know how to shoot it," she confessed with a sob.

"I'm hoping you won't need to."

They sat back to back in silence, each praying to survive their mission. The longer they waited, the more tense Clare grew. When Diana screamed, she leaped to her feet as Jeb tied the reins and jumped to the ground.

They were halted in their attempt at rescue by the sound of hooves thundering down the narrow road. It took only a second for Clare to recognize the trio bearing down upon them.

"Quick, inside! Diana just screamed!" she shouted. Jeb gathered the reins of the three abandoned horses and moved back to the heads of his well-trained team.

He grinned up at his companion. "We can sit tidy, now, Miss Seaton. His lordship will settle things all right and tight."

Clare could only pray he knew what he was talking about.

THE THREE MEN rushed into chaos. Lester had struggled to his feet and was battling four of the customers of The Royal Goose. Several others held a struggling Diana as they cheered on their compatriots. The roar of a pistol brought stillness to the room.

Richard, fire in his eyes, advanced menacingly on the two slovenly men clutching his wife. "Unhand the lady at once," he demanded in a steely voice. The pistol in his hand was no more threatening than his mien. As the two men debated their decision, a voice from the back of the room called out, "It's the Cap'n!"

A murmur ran through the group, but Richard ignored everything but Diana. "Let go of her," he repeated.

"If that's the Cap'n's lady, best turn 'er loose, lads. 'E'll tear you limb from limb to protect what's 'is, just like 'e did them Frogs."

The men took their hands off Diana. She stiffened her legs, afraid she'd fall and shame her husband, but she managed to walk, albeit awkwardly, over to the man who had now saved her life a second time.

"Who's back there?" Richard asked, acknowledging he'd heard the voice that had identified him even as he wrapped his left arm about Diana and pulled her tightly against him.

"It's me, Cap'n, Joseph Black," a scrawny little man called cheerfully, shoving his way through the motley crowd.

"Corporal Black," Richard replied. "I thank you for your assistance. If you will report to my house tomorrow, I would like to thank you again."

"'Tisn't necessary, Cap'n. Ye saved me many a time over the Channel."

"Are there others of our company here?" Richard listened as several voices answered. "If you won't come to me, I'll be back here tomorrow at two. Round up those you can find who need assistance."

Richard ignored his wife's moan of protest. He handed his pistol to Robert and swept Diana up into his arms. Without another word, he left the inn, followed by his friends and a bruised Lester.

As soon as they reached a safer neighbourhood, Richard called to Jeb to halt the carriage. He and his friends had been riding guard around the carriage, but he kept his eyes averted from his wife. Diana, watching him constantly, recognized that fact and despaired of his ever speaking to her again.

"Jeb, take my horse and ride to Doctor Brownell's. I'll drive the carriage the rest of the way back. Ask the doctor to come at once."

"I don't need—" Diana began, only to have Richard finally look at her with a burning glare that reduced her to silence. She huddled next to Clare, tears seeping through her tightly shut eyes.

They proceeded to their residence with no other words spoken. When Richard halted the carriage in front of the house, the door opened at once and Boswell and several footmen rushed down the stairs.

"My lord, where is Jeb?" Boswell couldn't help but ask. They had grown old together in the master's service.

"Gone to fetch the doctor. One of you come and take the reins." After he had relinquished them to the footman, Richard jumped down and opened the door to the barouche. Without comment, he gathered Diana into his arms and carried her up the steps. Robert slid from his horse and came to assist Clare. Edward followed the pair into the house.

Boswell showed the trio into the parlour. He would have preferred to accompany his master up the stairs to discover his mistress's state of health, but he knew his duty. Within minutes, he was serving his master's guests hot tea and brandy.

Clare, asked to pour out, nervously did so. Neither of the gentlemen spoke to her. Finally, unable to bear the silence any longer, she said, "What did they do to Diana?"

Robert jumped to his feet and stomped to the window, his back to her. Edward said, "I believe she is only bruised."

"It is a wonder both of you are not dead!" Robert shouted, his anger released from its fragile control.

Clare gasped and Edward protested his harsh words.

"How could you have been so foolish?" he demanded, ignoring his friend and concentrating on the most important woman in the world to him.

"We—we thought you were in trouble," Clare whispered.

Robert stared at her, his anger unappeased. "So you thought two women could rescue a couple of cripples?"

Clare's head came up, anger infusing strength in her. "We thought we might be able to assist you. Diana was going to go alone, but I would not hear of it. Were you as hale and hearty as oxen, we would have gone. Because we are stupid enough to care about you, you...you bacon-brained man!" She buried her face in her hands as tears ran down her cheeks.

Edward watched in silent amazement, unsure whether to intervene or not.

Robert forgot the existence of his friend as he dropped onto his knees in front of the weeping Clare. "My little love, don't you know that I am not worth such sacrifice?" His hands closed over hers and drew them from her face.

Her heart in her eyes, Clare leaned towards him to whisper, "You are worth any sacrifice, Robert. I love you with all my heart."

With a groan, Robert took her into his arms, his kiss answering her words. The next several minutes were heaven for the delirious couple before Edward decided Sara would expect his intervention.

"Ahem." The couple jumped apart. "May I assume you are making an offer for my sister-in-law, Sir Robert? I believe propriety would require it after the past few minutes."

Robert reached out a shaking hand to caress Clare's cheek. "I would give everything I own to wed Clare."

"Your heart is all I desire," she assured him, moving into his arms once more.

"Now, Clare, Sara will have my head if I don't chaperon you properly. We'll post the banns as soon as possible, but that's enough of that for now."

"Go away, Edward," Robert said, his eyes never leaving his loved one.

"PREPARE YOUR MISTRESS for bed," Richard growled as he relinquished his wife to her maid. "The doctor will be arriving any moment."

He stepped back out of the room, unable to be near her any longer. Leaning against the wall, he tried to remain calm, waiting for the doctor to arrive.

Doctor Brownell raced up the steps, the coachman having informed him of as much as he knew. Lord Rossley followed him into his wife's chamber and waited silently in the corner of the room. When the doctor had finished his examination, Lord Rossley led the way into the hallway. "Well?"

"Her ladyship is bruised and clearly shaken by what has happened, but there is nothing seriously wrong."

"Thank you, Doctor."

Though he gave his host a questioning look, there were no explanations before the butler, following his master's orders, showed him out to examine Lester. Richard, still standing in the hall, sagged against the wall. She would be all right.

Now his only difficulty was his own pain. How had it happened? He had intended to remain distant from his wife. To love anyone again was foolhardy. But Diana, sweet Diana, had made it impossible to ignore her. She had calmly stolen his heart.

Perhaps if he did not go near her, the feeling would subside, go away. Otherwise, he would again be as vulnerable to pain as he had been in his first marriage. *Except Diana is more trustworthy,* a little voice whispered.

That had not stopped her from frightening him today. If he had arrived a few minutes later, she might have been seriously injured, or even killed. No, it would be better to squelch this feeling before it took over his life. He would *not* love the delightful Diana, no matter how much he wanted to.

"I'M HUNGRY, Mama." Melly's piping voice wakened Diana from her dark thoughts.

"I'm sorry, darling. We stayed overlong at Sara's. We shall be home soon."

"Will my dress be pretty?"

"Oh, yes, sweetheart. You and Sally will be the most beautiful flower girls ever. The rose silk will be exquisite with your blond curls," Diana assured her companion. She had spent the afternoon assisting in the planning of Clare and Robert's wedding. She was happy the couple had discovered their love for each other. It was one of the few good things to come out of the fiasco she had created.

"What colour will your dress be, Mama?" Melly asked, pulling on Diana's sleeve to bring her back to her. Lately, Mama had been distracted all the time.

"What? Oh, it will be a darker rose, Melly."

They rode along in silence and Diana's thoughts returned to the results of her attempt to rescue her husband. Since their return, Lord Rossley had avoided her completely. The only news she had received of him was from Doctor Brownell. She had not even realized he used his left hand to hold and carry her that fateful evening, but after examining him and listening to her story, Doctor Brownell had concluded that her husband now had the use of that arm.

So Lord Rossley was well again. And she was sick almost to death with regret. Not because of his recovery; she gave grateful thanks for that. But because she had thrown away any hope of her husband's loving her. She had only wanted to keep him safe, and instead she had lost him.

"Mama, why are you so sad?"

Diana looked down at the little girl and reached over and hugged her. "I—I am just tired, my love."

"You need your tea," Melly said, nodding in agreement with her pronouncement. "I shall let you share my nursery tea, if you like." Her generosity was followed by an intent stare to see if she had convinced her mama to join her.

"Thank you, darling. I should love to." There was no need to concern herself with Richard. He would not take tea with her if Prinny himself were to command it.

The carriage stopped and the two Rossley ladies went up the steps hand in hand. The door was swung open sharply and they entered to find Lord Rossley advancing towards them, a glowering frown on his face.

"Where have you been?" he demanded.

"At Sara's," Diana replied, her eyes wide in astonishment.

"You were supposed to have returned over an hour ago!" Richard shouted, grabbing her shoulders and shaking her.

"Papa!" Melly protested, inserting herself between the two adults. "You mustn't hurt Mama!"

Stunned, Richard stared down at his child. "Hurt— of course not, Melly. I would never do such a thing."

"Mama is tired and sad," Melly explained, tilting her head back as she looked up at her father. "I shall let her share my nursery tea so she'll feel better."

Richard's hands fell from Diana's shoulders and he stepped back. His loss of control had shaken him. Kneeling down beside his young child, he said, "If I am sad also, may I share your nursery tea?"

Melly reached and gently patted her father's shoulder. "Of course you may, Papa. I shall take care of you."

Richard looked up at Diana. "May I join you, my lady?"

Since these were his first words to her, other than his angry welcome, in several days, Diana stared at him in surprise. When she realized her family was awaiting a response, she nodded. So all three Rossleys, linked by Melly's handholding, proceeded up the stairs to take nursery tea.

CHAPTER FIFTEEN

MELLY CHATTERED all through tea, but her guests were noticeably silent. She told her father all about the gown she would wear as flower girl and how much Nicholas detested being in the wedding. She explained that she was bigger than Sally, so she had to tell Sally what to do. She even revealed that Sally and Nicholas were going to get a baby. Nothing moved either of her guests to respond. They sat in silence, carefully avoiding each other's eyes.

"I've changed my mind, Papa," Melly finally said.

"What?" Richard asked, frowning, his concentration all on the woman sitting across from him.

"I've changed my mind," Melly repeated patiently, reaching over to pat her father's hand.

He covered her small hand with his large one and carried it to his lips, a half smile on his face. "What have you changed your mind about, my child?"

"A baby."

Neither adult responded, though Melly noticed how tightly her father was clutching her hand.

"If Nicholas is going to get a baby, Papa, I must have one. If not, he will boast all the time."

"I see. And are you not concerned that Mama might forget you if she has a baby?"

"No. Mama has promised to love me, and she always keeps her promises." Melly jumped up to embrace Diana, who returned the hug but kept her eyes averted.

"How true," Lord Rossley murmured, while he stared at his wife. As her cheeks blossomed with colour, Richard stood. "Lady Melanie, I ask that you excuse Lady Rossley and myself," he said formally, bowing to the little girl. "We must confer on several matters of great importance."

Melly giggled at her father's play-acting, missing the startled look on Diana's face. "All right, Papa. Will you discuss the baby? I would like to have mine before Nicholas, please."

"Er, we shall see, my dear."

Once the two adults were in the hall with the door closed behind them, Richard murmured, "In the study, please, my dear."

Diana preceded her husband down the stairs, her knees shaking with every step. What did he intend to say? He had avoided her since their venture to The Royal Goose. Was he now going to reprimand her? Or was he going to take the drastic step of divorcing her? Diana steeled herself to accept his decision with equanimity.

"I wish to apologize for my harsh welcome this afternoon," he finally said after she was seated. He paced across the room as he spoke. "I—I find myself worrying about you when your movements are unaccounted for.''

''But I told Boswell I would be at Sara's,'' Diana replied, surprise in her voice.

''But you were late!'' Richard returned.

''I—I'm sorry. We were planning the wedding and I did not notice the time.''

Noting her confusion and surprise, Richard turned his back upon her. ''Yes, of course.''

When he remained silent, Diana at last found the courage to speak. ''I have been intending to apologize for... for my involving all of us in that regrettable event, R-Richard,'' she said, faltering when he turned to glare at her.

Her pale cheeks silenced his first impulse to respond in anger. He grudgingly said, ''I must share the blame. I had intended to explain about Mad Molly, but... I became distracted from my purpose,'' he finished, as both thought of the sweet distraction which had taken place in that very room.

Tears started in Diana's eyes as she remembered the hopes and dreams that embrace had awakened. ''No, it is my fault. You had warned me against interfering in your activities. I will accept whatever punishment you wish to give me.''

''Why did you go there, Diana? Didn't you know how dangerous it would be?'' Richard demanded, asking the question that had bothered him for several days.

Averting her eyes, she whispered, ''I thought you were in danger.''

Richard crossed the room and again seized his wife by her shoulders, but this time gently, pulling her from the sofa. "My dear, you might have been seriously injured, or worse. You should never have put yourself in such danger."

Diana stared up into his bright blue eyes, the tears that had earlier filled her own spilling over onto her pale cheeks. "I could not—"

"What?" Richard asked when she broke off.

"I could not believe you in danger and do nothing."

Her tragic face was more than Richard could bear. He wrapped both arms about her and brought her trembling body to rest against his. Stroking her hair, he whispered, "Not all bad came from that night. Robert and Clare are to be married—and I have regained the use of my arm."

"I know," Diana whispered into his cravat. "I am so h-happy for you."

"Something else may be attributed to our time at The Royal Goose," Richard said, holding her even tighter.

Diana leaned back against his arms, her tear-stained face turned up to his. "What?"

With a groan, his lips crushed hers as he gave in to the desires her closeness inflamed. Diana, having longed to touch him, to hold him, since that morning, wrapped her arms tightly round his neck and pressed against him. She had thought he would never embrace her again.

When the kiss ended, both were trembling. Diana slowly relaxed her arms, but Richard pulled her tight against him again. "Do not go away. I must explain what else good came from our escapade."

"Yes?" Diana asked, distracted by the warmth of him and the rising desire she felt.

"I discovered that I had no choice about loving you."

Diana stood as if turned to stone, staring up at him.

"I never intended to care for you at all, my love. I didn't want to be hurt again," he explained. "But you are so sweet, so good, I wanted to be with you more and more. Then, after our kiss that morning, I thought—I thought I would treat you as my mistress," he confessed, his face red.

Diana buried her face against his chest, hiding the desire that flared up within her, even as she hoped for more.

"But the thought that you might be in danger destroyed all my illusions. I discovered that I already loved you. It was too late to protect myself from your sweetness."

"But you have avoided me since our return!" Diana protested, her voice filled with the pain his rejections caused.

"I know, my love. I thought...if I avoided you, perhaps my emotions would subside," he explained, a rueful smile on his face. "Instead, my feelings for you have daily grown stronger until they could not be denied. I have been aware of your every movement since our brief visit to The Royal Goose. When you did not return at the appointed hour today, I could not restrain my fear of losing you.''

With a sob, Diana lifted her head to smile blindingly at her beloved husband. ''Oh, Richard, I love you so! I thought you would never forgive me for interfering.''

''I forgave you at once. But I fought against surrendering to my feelings,'' he explained as his lips met hers once more.

A few minutes later, seated on the sofa with his wife in his arms, Richard whispered, ''Can you ever forgive me for my difficult behaviour?'' Since he accompanied his question with a long kiss that drew a sigh of contentment from Diana, it took several moments to answer.

''I must forgive you anything, my love,'' she confessed. ''Not only are you a war hero, but you have also saved my life not once, but twice.''

''I believe, madam wife, that I prefer *your* manner of welcoming a hero to that of Society,'' he teased.

''Just wait, my lord,'' Diana daringly responded. ''I have only begun to welcome you home.'' She shivered in anticipation as Richard indicated his approval.

He drew back from her one last time. ''I believe we only have one issue left with which to deal.''

''What is that?''

''Who is to explain to Melly that no matter how hard we work at it, Nicholas will get his baby first?''

THIS JULY, HARLEQUIN OFFERS YOU THE PERFECT SUMMER READ!

Sunsational

EMMA DARCY
EMMA GOLDRICK
PENNY JORDAN
CAROLE MORTIMER

From top authors of Harlequin Presents comes HARLEQUIN SUNSATIONAL, a four-stories-in-one book with 768 pages of romantic reading.

Written by such prolific Harlequin authors as Emma Darcy, Emma Goldrick, Penny Jordan and Carole Mortimer, HARLEQUIN SUNSATIONAL is the perfect summer companion to take along to the beach, cottage, on your dream destination or just for reading at home in the warm sunshine!

Don't miss this unique reading opportunity.

Available wherever Harlequin books are sold.

Back by Popular Demand

Janet Dailey

Americana

A romantic tour of America through fifty favorite Harlequin
Presents, each set in a different state researched by Janet
and her husband, Bill. A journey of a lifetime in one
cherished collection.

In July, don't miss the exciting states featured in:

Title #11 — HAWAII
Kona Winds

#12 — IDAHO
The Travelling Kind

*Available wherever
Harlequin books are sold.*

HARLEQUIN

Romance

**This June, travel to Turkey
with Harlequin Romance's**

**THE JEWELS OF HELEN
by Jane Donnelly**

She was a spoiled brat who liked her own way.

Eight years ago Max Torba thought Anni was self-centered—
and that she didn't care if her demands made life impossible
for those who loved her.

Now, meeting again at Max's home in Turkey, it was clear he
still held the same opinion, no matter how hard she tried to
make a good impression. ''You haven't changed much, have
you?'' he said. ''You still don't give a damn for the trouble you
cause.''

But did Max's opinion really matter? After all, Anni had no
intention of adding herself to his admiring band of female
followers....

Take 4 bestselling love stories FREE

Plus get a FREE surprise gift!

Harlequin Superromance®

CHILDREN OF THE HEART
by Sally Garrett

Available this August

Romance readers the world over have wept and
rejoiced over Sally Garrett's heartwarming stories of
love, caring and commitment. In her new novel,
Children of the Heart, Sally once again weaves a story
that will touch your most tender emotions.

You'll be moved to tears of joy

Nearly two hundred children have passed through
Trenance McKay's foster home. But after her husband
leaves her, Trenance knows she'll always have to
struggle alone. No man could have enough room in his
heart both for Trenance and for so many needy
children. Max Tulley, news anchor for KSPO TV is
willing to try, but how long can his love last?

"Sally Garrett does some of the best character studies
in the genre and will not disappoint her fans."
Romantic Times

**Look for *Children of the Heart* wherever
Harlequin Romance novels are sold.** SCH-1